Marieta Louise McMillen

Other books by M. L. Spurgeon in
order of publication

death is Belligerent
death is Compulsive
death is Deafening
death is Equestrian
death is Always With Us
death is a Fumbler

Dueling Sisters: Seasons of Change
a book of Poetry

Death in a Green House

a John Holmes Johnson Mystery

M. L. Spurgeon

authorHOUSE®

AuthorHouse™
1663 Liberty Drive
Bloomington, IN 47403
www.authorhouse.com
Phone: 1-800-839-8640

© 2012 M. L. Spurgeon. All rights reserved.

No part of this book may be reproduced, stored in a retrieval system, or transmitted by any means without the written permission of the author.

Published by AuthorHouse 9/18/2012

ISBN: 978-1-4685-2773-5 (sc)
ISBN: 978-1-4685-2772-8 (e)

Library of Congress Control Number: 2011962578

Any people depicted in stock imagery provided by Thinkstock are models, and such images are being used for illustrative purposes only.
Certain stock imagery © Thinkstock.

This book is printed on acid-free paper.

Because of the dynamic nature of the Internet, any web addresses or links contained in this book may have changed since publication and may no longer be valid. The views expressed in this work are solely those of the author and do not necessarily reflect the views of the publisher, and the publisher hereby disclaims any responsibility for them.

To my brothers

Lee and John

"Thou puttest my feet also in
the stocks, and lookest narrowly
unto all my paths; thou settest
a print upon the heels of my feet."

Job 13:27 (KJV)

Prologue

I have kept journals ever since my brother opened the Holmes Detective Agency in 1940. It was as natural for me to write about my brother's adventures as it had become to write about my estate, my wife and my children. I wrote down the facts accumulated from my conversations with my brother, John Holmes, and information from his investigating detectives. I learned more from my occasional participation and personal conversations. It was no surprise that I soon became the official chronicler of the exploits of the Holmes Detective Agency.

Eventually I began to put my material into book form, changing names here and there to protect identities. It had been suggested by one of my twins when he turned fifteen.

And so I shall continue as long as I am able.

Jonothan Patrick Overly II

John Holmes Johnson mystery #7
Major Players

Residents and co-owners of the Overly estate:
   Narrator: Jonothan Patrick Overly II   b. in Kansas City Mo.
        his wife: Carrie Jean (Webb)
        twins: Hudson and Sanford 3 ½
        daughters: Lori Marie 1 ½ and Hannah Elisabeth 3 mo.

Patrick's foster brother: John Holmes Johnson   b. in England
        his wife: Samantha Louise

Overly estate staff:
        Butler: Jon Davis
        his wife: Jennifer, nanny for the Overly children
        sons: Sean and Colin Douglas-Davis 9
               b. in England (survived the London blitz)
        Maid: Irene Keene
        Cook: Janis Jacoby
        groundskeeper: Kendall Wiles
        Stableman: Owen Farmer and his sons:
        sons: Olson and Phillip
        Mechanic: Ian Reilly
        Gardeners: Washington and his wife, Sue Foster
        Live-in help for John Holmes and Samantha:
               Malcolm and Marian Macdougal

Holmes Detective Agency with offices in KCMO:
        director: John Holmes
        #1 Detective: Malcolm Macdougal   b. in Scotland
        his wife: Marian
        #2 Detective: George St. Giles   b. in England
        his wife: Georganne
        #3 Detective: William Leonard
        his wife: Mollie
        his sons: triplets

        Other Detectives featured:
        KCKPD: Edwin Vernon and partner, Lee Emerson
        KCMO: Robert Wright
        KCMO: Charlie Raymond and partner, Innes Wallace

Contents

Prologue vii

Chapter one
    Death is Green December 25-26, 1942 1

Chapter two
    See the Forest December 26-28, 1942 17

Chapter three
    Metal Rods and Sandpaper December 26, 1942 ... 33

Chapter four
    A Common Denominator December 28 & 29, 1942 ... 43

Chapter five
    A Meeting of Minds December 29 & 30, 1942 ... 56

Chapter six
    Families in Crisis December 31, 1942-January 1, 1943 ... 67

Chapter seven
    Extenuating Circumstances January 1-7, 1943 ... 74

Chapter eight
    Out of the Blue January 7 & 8, 1943 95

Chapter nine
    Cobwebs January 8-11, 1943 110

Chapter ten
    Two Blind Mice January 13-15, 1943 123

Chapter eleven
    Day Dreamer January 15-20, 1943   **143**

Chapter twelve
    The Blizzard January 14-18, 1943   **149**

Chapter thirteen
    One Family January 19, 1943   **161**

Chapter fourteen
    The Sins of the Fathers January 20-27, 1943   **172**

Chapter fifteen
    Pulling it Together January 27, 1943   **185**

Epilogue   **193**

Scottish to English   **195**

Coincidences
Wrapped in the green of surprise
Murder strikes across state lines
Engaging many actors
One big ball of yarn

Chapter one

Death is Green
December 25-26, 1942

It was Christmas 1942.

The United States of America had been at war for twelve months. There was some rationing; sugar, coffee, and gasoline for example, and American plants were producing war-related goods; military vehicles instead of cars, bombers and fighters instead of DC-3's and light aircraft.

In June of that year President Roosevelt had called on the nation to collect and turn in rubber of all descriptions. Within the first four weeks, the appeal had gathered in some 450,000 tons. Other campaigns followed.

In the middle of an article about the assassination of Admiral Darlan in France, I laid the newspaper aside to greet my sister-in-law, Samantha Louise Johnson. We exchanged pecks on the cheeks and she moved on to greet my wife, Carrie Jean. The cousins hugged.

I silently thanked God as I sat amidst the cheerful warmth of fireplace and Christmas tree with its towers of gifts spilling out in all directions.

I had four children. My daughter Lori Marie, 1 ½, was sitting on her Grandma Anna's lap. Hudson was on the floor by her knee and Sanford sat next to her while she read the ever popular, 'The Night Before Christmas'. The twins were 3 ½. Hannah Elisabeth at three months, was our youngest. She was happily engaged in entertaining her grandfather, Frank Webb.

I was very proud of my family.

I must have sighed because a voice to my right spoke, and a hand touched my shoulder.

"Everything all right, Patrick?"

"Absolutely, Joel. Just admiring the view, you know?" I swept my arm to take in the beautiful scene.

My brother-in-law chuckled. "It is indeed beautiful."

"What's beautiful, darling?" Adele Belle kissed her husband's cheek as she said it and batted her long eyelashes at him.

He replied with the expected answer just as his 22-month-old climbed onto his lap energetically.

"Well, hello Samuel Benjamin Anderson. Where have you been?"

The baby chortled happily as his daddy tickled him.

"He was with us, Joel," said a new voice.

Maria and Joseph Billings came into the room with their two children. Harold Steven was two, Donald Silas one.

Maria addressed Adele. "I changed my two and Samuel wanted his diaper freshened, so I obliged."

"Thank you, darling."

"Where is Sarah?" asked Joseph.

"Right here, sound asleep." Adele pointed to the floor next to the sofa. The seven-month-old was in a basket, smiling contentedly in her sleep.

"She looks happy enough." Joseph sat down beside me. "If this family keeps growing, Patrick, you will need a larger living room."

You could knock out a wall," added Adele.

"Quite right. Splendid suggestion."

This voice had an English accent.

Every eye in the room turned to watch my long-time butler, Jon Davis pushing my foster brother's wheelchair through the wide door.

Lori Marie clapped her hands joyfully to see her uncle.

John Holmes Johnson nodded his head her way so she giggled.

Samuel clapped, so Holmes tipped his head at him. Of course, my twins had to get in on the act too.

By now the room was filled with happy laughter.

Samantha met the wheelchair mid-room and kissed her husband.

He playfully touched her tummy. "It won't be long you realize, our baby is due in March. He may be the straw that…"

I held up my hand. "Spare me the old cliché about the camel, Holmes. Where are the Macdougal's?"

"On their way. They are bringing our gifts to add to that awesome pile." Holmes looked around the room. "Where shall we put Malcolm? He is a big 6'4". Why, he is nearly as tall as that tree." His eyes followed the tree up its ten feet to the tip, adorned with a golden star. "I am impressed."

Samantha moved her husband to one side of the room and sat down in a hard-backed chair to his left.

"Let me see, who are we missing?" I mused aloud. "Jon and Jenny Davis, and those two rascals, oh my, what are their names?" I tapped my forehead and screwed up my face.

Sanford and Hudson mimicked me.

Two young scalawags burst through the door with theatrical flair.

"Sean!" He went to one knee; arms outstretched like a young Al Jolson.

"And Colin!" He went down beside his twin brother.

"And here's mother" they exclaimed dramatically.

Jennifer Jamison Davis came into view and leaned her slightly heavy body against the doorjamb, looking surprisingly provocative. She cooed softly,

"I'm here boys. What'l It be?"

Jon Davis closed his eyes in mock embarrassment; the ten-year-old boys from England rolled on the floor, laughing.

The room was filled with sounds of merriment.

Marian walked in with arms full of packages and tripped over Colin.

There was instant silence, the last note of gaiety effectively reverberating in the room as twelve adults and eight children watched the slow motion fall of Marian Macdougal, age 60. Packages slid across the room.

As swiftly as the crisis started, it was over.

Joseph Billings jumped from his chair and grabbed the falling woman, who then landed gently on the floor, cushioned by the small but sturdy boy.

Jenny had stopped Malcolm at the door where they had helplessly watched the drama unfold.

Marian began to laugh as she rolled off Colin Davis. She tousled his curly hair and they shared a hug.

The doctor declared no one hurt and a collective sigh of relief went around the room.

Sean and Colin scurried about picking up gifts and placing them under the Christmas tree.

Joseph took the two cloth shopping bags from Malcolm, handing them to Colin.

The big Scotsman put his long arms around his wife.

Awakened by the sudden burst of nervous laughter, which

pierced the silent tension, Sarah Samantha Anderson began to wail.

"See what ye did, lo'e? Ye woke the wee one." There was brave sensitivity to the voice. Malcolm Macdougal kissed his wife firmly.

"Are ye hale, lass? Ye shouldna gie me gliff."

"Aye, ye sonsy mon. Were ye rad?"

"That I was, my gudewife."

I had walked up behind the couple and now I put my arms around them. I kissed Marian's cheek. "Come sit, dear lady. We saved seats for you two next to Holmes, unless of course, you would like to get away from the mon, awee?" I grinned foolishly at Malcolm's hearty laugh.

The man slapped my back at which I made a loud, woof" and peals of childish laughter rang out. I staggered to the piano while Malcolm escorted his wife to her seat.

Sarah was contentedly occupied with nursing, discreetly covered by a lap blanket, while big brother, Samuel, looked on.

The wall clock said 7:00 o'clock p.m. We had sung at least six Christmas Carols before we heard the doorbell. We listened to our maid, Irene, answer the door. Two minutes later we were greeting Pastor John Stephens with a rousing chorus of, "For he's a jolly good fellow."

After greetings all around, he went to his unofficially adopted son, John Holmes Johnson.

Malcolm relinquished his seat so that the man could sit by the wheelchair. Malcolm grabbed an unoccupied footstool.

I played 'Greensleeves' while Colin sang "What Child is this" in his beautiful young tenor voice. The last note ebbed away. I closed the piano and returned to my chair. Carrie sat on my lap.

The room grew quiet with anticipation.

Irene Keene, our maid, and Janis Jacoby, our wonderful

cook, slipped into the room and sat on a bench by my wife and I. We all listened to the old familiar Christmas story that never truly got old. John Stephens closed his well-used Bible and offered a prayer.

It was time. The children could barely maintain their composure. Joel had his ever-present camera ready.

Carrie and Jenny took their places by the Christmas tree, facing a half-circle of eager children seated on the floor in front of them.

Carrie picked up the first package and you could hear the air sucked in, everyone waiting to see who got the very first present. Jenny discreetly laid packages in a row to make sure each child got one.

With flair, Carrie handed the first gift to Samuel and he hammed it up for his father's camera.

The two youngest stayed on adult laps, Sarah on her mother's and Hannah on her grandfather's.

In minutes all the children were ripping open their first gift. There were appropriate sounds of appreciation all around.

Soon each adult had presents on his or her lap too. For a while at least, we all forgot about the devastation of London, the war with Japan, and the equally ugly war against evil my brother's detective agency fought daily.

By now it was 11:00 o'clock; the infants were sound asleep, each one in his or her mother's arms and the toddlers were all yawning.

Maria and Marian picked up the torn pieces of paper, carefully folding those salvageable, to save. No one knew what state our economy might be in by next Christmas so we chose to join the ranks of the frugal.

Irene brought in cider and Christmas cookies followed by coffee and spiced tea.

"Whoops," said my wife suddenly.

All eyes turned her way.

"I see a package in the back that we missed. Get it for me will you, Sean?"

He happily crawled under the tree.

Carrie tried to read the tag. She shook her head and passed it to me. I shook my head. Joel couldn't read it either, nor could Adele.

"Let me see that," said Colin Douglas. The fourth grader looked at it carefully, and then he laughed. "It's not for anyone in the room, that's why you couldn't decipher it." He got up from the floor and walked to the wheelchair. Handing the gift to Holmes, he explained. "It's for Titus and Trouble, Sir."

"Go on," said Sean, "open it!"

Holmes looked at the two huge rawhide chews on his lap. He picked one up and sniffed it. "Smells delicious. Thank you boys. My wolfhounds will love them. Especially Trouble, who chews on everything." He rolled his eyes, a gesture that was rewarded with childish giggles.

Many minutes of contented time ticked by.

Adele Bell Anderson sighed.

Sarah Samantha stirred a bit but did not wake up. Adele gently rocked her in her arms.

Joel looked at his wife and nodded.

"This has been so lovely, darlings, but we must go. Joel is on call tomorrow. I pray that there are no murders for the next few days and nights."

Carrie brought coats and buntings. Adele bundled the sleeping baby while Joel tackled the exhausted, almost asleep, Samuel.

Pastor Stephens followed them out, and then the Billings family left.

The room was decidedly emptier when all the women still present, went upstairs with the four Overly youngsters.

I looked around my living room reflectively.

There was something sad about all the empty chairs and a rug littered with toys but no children.

"Aye, tis indeed a waeful sight."

"Quite right, my friend." John Holmes could not quite stifle the yawn that forced its way out. "I do believe that I am as tired as they are." He tipped his head toward Sean and Colin, stretched out on the carpet.

"Perhaps I better head them toward our apartment, I admit, I'm a wee tired myself." Jon Davis grinned at Malcolm.

"When do you leave for Springfield, Malcolm?"

"After breakfast, Patrick, ten or so. I am vera anxious to see the bairns." The big man ran his hand through his thick, gray hair. "I am a vera sonsy mon the day with a waly family I thought I wad ne'er hae..." his voice trailed away.

I was happy for him. He had come to America before the war broke out, staying with a cousin, Doctor Howard Hayden. The sixty-one-year-old was a retired Scotland Yard detective, never married. He had been seriously wounded and was unable to father children so he had refused to burden a woman with "half a mon" as he had put it. Marian had changed his mind. They were happily married, and together they looked after my brother and his wife.

"Mildred and Jeff seem to like you, Malcolm, and their two boys love having you for their grandfather. I can tell," said Samantha as she entered the room. She kissed his forehead.

Marian followed her example but she kissed him twice. "Shall we go then, lo'e?"

"Aye, Mrs. Macdougal. Loot us get these daft callants hame to bed. We hae a vera canty day tomorrow." He stood and stretched his lean, tall body. "It's already been gude days, more to com."

I helped Davis with his sleepy boys and we all filed out of the room.

Carrie and Jenny were upstairs with the children. When

I returned, Jenny would join her family for a well-deserved rest.

It had indeed been a grand Christmas.

"Tomorrow is Saturday," my wife mumbled into my ear as we snuggled under the quilts. I fell asleep in the middle of my prayer.

*****

Something tickled my face and I tried to brush it away. It tickled my cheek again. Thinking it to be a fly that had somehow escaped its demise, I was contemplating whether or not it was worth the effort to wake up in order to eliminate the nuisance, when the warm hand of my wife slid inside my pajama top.

"Good morning-after-Christmas, Jonothan Patrick Overly, Jr."

She kissed my chin. Her hand moved and my eyes opened.

"What time is it?"

"Why?"

Around kisses, I managed to gasp out, "No reason."

Time slipped by as it has a habit of doing, while we gave each other one more Christmas present. Light slowly filtered into the room around the drapes, chasing away the shadows. Carrie lay quietly in my arms and twisted the kinky hair on my abdomen in the vicinity of my belly button.

"Are ye sonsy, my love?" I asked, borrowing a phrase from Malcolm.

"Aye, darling. I am very happy. My sister, Adele is happy, my cousin, Samantha is happy, your brother is happy..." she stopped.

I realized that she was crying.

"What is it, Carrie?" I kissed her forehead.

"I'm sorry, Patrick. I am so happy, that I am afraid."

"Be ye not afraid, but put your trust in the Lord."

My wife giggled. "I don't think that is an accurate quote, my darling."

"Sorry."

We were kissing again, her salty tears gracing my lips, when sudden high-pitched wails bounced off the walls.

"Your daughter, darling."

"You go get her, love. I'm naked."

This time I chuckled. "I'm naked too, darling, however…" I jumped out of bed and grabbed my robe. My wife swatted my bottom with a resounding slap.

"Ouch."

Carrie slipped past me headed for the bathroom; I picked up our tiny blond with the very big voice.

I walked into the master bedroom and opened the drapes. "It's snowing," I announced as I watched Malcolm Macdougal bring two suitcases out of their apartment and put them in the trunk of my brother's black sedan.

Hannah was sucking on my robe when her fully dressed mother took her from me. I dressed.

Breakfast was proceeding according to plan when the telephone rang.

"For you, sir, its Marian from the residence."

As I walked to the hall phone, I reminisced about the reason we called it the residence, remembering the day my brother had broached the idea of remodeling the cottage behind the main house into a bachelor home. He had enlarged it and added a deck. Since then it had grown and changed, reaching its limits for expansion. Now, of course, it was no longer a bachelor's quarters.

I picked up the telephone. Carrie had followed me and stood by my side, cradling a contented Hannah Elisabeth

The baby burped loudly just as I said, Hello, Marian."

There was a merry laugh from her end of the line.

"Sorry, that was Hannah."

"We are leaving, Patrick, and just wanted you to know. The radio says this snow will not accumulate. We will drive carefully, regardless." She paused.

I waited.

"And, Patrick…"

"Don't worry, Marian. We will take good care of Holmes and Samantha. No fretting and fashing. Tell that stubborn Scotsman of yours. Christmas greetings to your family. Here's Carrie."

After brief words with the kind grandmotherly lady, my wife hung up.

I stood at the window watching the car leave our driveway. Phillip Farmer ran out to the car as it stopped by the stable. His brother, Olsen, followed him. The two stable boys were very fond of the man. The car drove on and the boys waved.

I felt an arm go around my waist. I draped mine over my wife's shoulders. "What's the plan for today, darling?"

My wife laughed.

*****

Across the state line, at the western edge of an area known as Mission Hills, another man's wife laughed at the antics of her young grandson. The four-year-old rode a beautifully carved and polychrome hobbyhorse that he had gotten for Christmas. He looked splendid in his new blue-green cowboy outfit that was complete with chaps and boots. There were no spurs, of course, nor did the boy have guns.

Genevieve Mary-Margaret Greene, wife of the Honorable Leroy Elliot Justin Greene, sat in a luxuriously appointed living room, filled with elegant furniture.

She was a vibrant, lean, and athletic six feet tall. From her close-cropped silver hair to her toes, she looked the part. She had been excellent at tennis, swimming, horseback riding, and skiing, all of her 61 years.

The woman's green eyes misted as she gazed beyond the boy and out the huge window at her vast estate. Beside her stood a walker, needed since a fall from an unruly horse one year ago today.

The antebellum, two story, twenty-two room mansion and its outbuildings huddled in the geographical center of the 340 acre estate grounds, occupying a mere 1200 square-feet. It was painted three shades of green, the main color being a light gray-green that was easy on the eyes. The heavy, decorative trim was lime tinted white as were the 30 pillars. The five porches and all of the balustrades were a darker green.

The house was surrounded by an immaculate lawn that stretched on and on with a row of stately oak trees lining the long, main driveway.

There were three other driveways, each with a massive gate, also green.

The front lawn was an unbroken expanse of grass bordered with a wrought iron fence.

Behind the house was an elaborate garden, old-world style, laid out like a miniature Versailles. Eight hundred feet east of the exact center of the property was a three-car garage housing three blue-green Cadillacs and eight hundred feet west, was a circular greenhouse.

Behind the garage was a stable where four American Quarter-horses, two Arabians, and a pony resided. Behind the greenhouse were tennis courts.

Beyond all these structures, lined up with the main house, were five attached cottage houses. They were built to match the elegance of the main structure, on a smaller scale. An estate staff of nine lived in the beautifully furnished cottages.

The whole layout was meticulously symmetrical.

Genevieve started as a voice spoke near her elbow.

"Are you well, mother?"

She took her eyes off the estate she so loved to look at her oldest son. She took his hand.

"Of course, Kenneth. I was simply admiring the garden. You know how much I love it."

"I know, darling." He kissed his mother's forehead lightly. "Has Elliot been entertaining you?"

"Absolutely! What a good horseman he is." Genevieve clapped her hands and said, "Bravo."

Elliot Willard, so named after her husband and his father, Willard Leroy, leaped from his wonderful mount and ran to kiss his Grandma Gen.

Kenneth Leroy Greene settled in a chair and opened the Kansas City morning newspaper. After reading four articles about various aspects of a nation at war, he stopped. He sat thinking about his four younger brothers, all in uniform and far away from home. Lincoln was a sailor on the USS Albacore, Melvin was in the Air Force flying a B52 in Europe, and both Noel and Paine were in the army somewhere in the South Pacific. At forty, Kenneth was the oldest, and not drafted.

His mother looked up when he sighed.

Elliot ran over to throw his arms around his father. There was a pervasive sadness about the house that the young boy did not understand.

"Where is grandpa?"

"In the greenhouse I suppose. It is his hide-away, Elliot, like the room in the attic where you like to play."

Kathleen Mair, 32, walked into the room carrying their two-year-old. Eveleen Rowena was named after her grandmother and great-grandmother, still living in Ireland. Her name meant pleasant and agreeable. So she was, as pleasant a child as you could hope for, and this despite her braces for the child had been born with a spinal defect. She could walk but only when wearing the heavy metal that encompassed her entire lower body from the waist down.

Kathleen lowered her daughter to the floor, and the towhead waddled to her Grandma Gen.

The child was all smiles and laughter. The mood lifted as Eveleen showed off her new dress, a Christmas present from her Aunt Blythe, wife of Noel Lorimer Greene.

Minutes later, Tyrone appeared at the door to announce lunch. The butler was 59. He and his wife, Carolyn, had been with the judge since 1906.

"Lunch is spread, madam. I sent my son to the greenhouse to inform Judge Greene."

"Thank you, Tyrone. You had a nice visit with your brother, I hope?"

"Most excellent Christmas, madam. Thank you, and thank you for the gifts." The man with prematurely white hair the color of bleached cotton, cleared his throat.

"What is it, Tyrone?" asked Kenneth.

"Well, sir, we would like you to know, should things become, difficult, we will stay with you regardless."

Kenneth looked at Tyrone Radburn Wells for several minutes, long enough that it made the man uneasy. He looked down at his shoes, afraid that he had somehow offended the family.

Kenneth Greene got up, walked to the butler and then took his hand. Shaking it firmly, he said, "Thank you, Tyrone. That is a comfort to me and I truly appreciate it. Times may indeed become hard before we see an end to this conflict."

"Kenneth!"

Kathleen's cry sent chills up her husband's spine. He turned to see Seadon Wells running full speed through the garden. The look on his face as he bounded across the wide porch was frightful.

The two men looked at the arched doorway where Seadon

now stood. His face was bleached of all color; he was shaking and breathing hard.

"My God, sir. Oh my God, sir."

"What is it, Seadon? Speak up." Kenneth put his hands on the twenty-six-year-old shoulders.

"Your father is dead. In the greenhouse."

Genevieve began to cry.

*****

In a modest green house on Sunset Drive off 52nd Street, another man's wife was crying over the death of her husband.

Eric Fritz Grun had supposedly committed suicide November twentieth by jumping from the roof of Union Station onto the tracks below.

Everyone was satisfied with that answer except Sandra Rose. She believed he had been murdered because of the prejudice of his fellow workers.

Her husband had been a gentle man, German in name only. He had been born and raised in Missouri, the child of a German father and an American mother. He was not, never had been, nor would he have ever become a Nazi, but only she knew that beyond a shadow of a doubt.

Mrs. Grun dabbed her eyes on her apron and picked up the telephone.

*****

Across State Line Road, east of the Greene mansion, at 75th and Grandview, a young man with an awkward gait approached the front door of a green stucco house. Behind him were his wife, Charlotte and their two children. He rang the doorbell several times and then got out his key. It was 1:30.

It would be a day David Ault Sloan would never forget. As

soon as the door opened, as he hesitated to pick up his sack of gifts, his two youngsters raced inside. "Grandma, grandma, we're here, grandma."

Smiling at Charlotte, David followed them in.

The happy, cheerfulness of Naomi Sue, eight, and the exuberance of four-year-old Daniel Dexter, was replaced by terrified screams.

Dropping his packages, David hurried as fast as his polio-weakened legs would carry him. Charlotte ran past him to gather her stricken children into her arms.

The family stared in disbelief at the bludgeoned body of Lucille Lydia Sloan.

It was Charlotte who called the police.

*****

By 2:30, six detectives were on their separate ways to look into three separate murders.

Detectives Edwin Wylie Vernon with his partner, Lee Emerson of the Kansas City, Kansas police department drove to the Greene mansion. Joel Jacob Anderson with Zeke Martin of the Kansas City, Missouri police headed for the Sloan home while John Holmes Johnson and his wife Samantha of the Holmes Detective Agency answered the call from Sandra Rose Grun.

At the base of trees
The drama of life and death-
Over and under the leaves
Myriad life forms struggle
On the forest floor

Chapter two

See the Forest
December 26-28, 1942

Saturday evening there was a second Christmas celebration with a smaller pile of gifts surrounding the tree.

Jon and Jenny Davis, with their two foster sons, had gone to Kansas City to spend the next two days with Jon's son, Jack, his wife, Judy, their daughter-in-law, Ruthie, and one-month-old Elette Jennifer Davis. The baby's father, George Davis, was in the service stationed in Ireland.

Also gone were Malcolm and Marian Macdougal.

Irene and Janis had stayed on through the holidays, having no other family nearby to celebrate with. Janis had lost her husband, Seth Jacoby, on the USS Perch. The submarine had been lost with all hands off Java in March.

Today we had a chance to let the staff know how much they were appreciated .

My brother had moved from Sussex, England in 1923 to live

at the Overly estate in Kansas City, Missouri, not because he did not like his homeland, far from it. It had been an adventure into a new, vibrant, and developing country. It had been a chance to have new experiences and to make new friends. He had gone to University in England and again, in the United States.

John Holmes had been young and athletic, strong, lean, and graceful in his movements. He had loved to hike, fish, camp, and ride horseback. That was before 1938.

I opened my eyes. I was sitting alone in the drawing room with the La-Z-Boy tilted back. The children were napping with Irene sitting in for the absent nanny. Carrie was helping the cook prepare for guests, to arrive at 6:00. I glanced at my watch. "Four more hours."

Shaking my head at the unbelievably melancholic mood I found myself in, I decided to go outside for a walk.

Once dressed appropriately in boots and overcoat, I went to the kitchen. My wife stood with her back to the door, making biscuits.

"Carrie?"

I guess there was something in the tone of my voice that alerted her, because she turned, wiped her hands on a towel, and stepped into my arms.

"What is it, Patrick?"

"I'm not sure, Carrie. I feel down and I don't understand why. I'm going to take a walk around."

We shared a kiss. "All right, darling."

"Smells wonderful, Janis. What are you cooking?"

"Ham, scalloped potatoes, green bean casserole…"

"Stop, stop." I laughed at the sudden hunger pang that threatened to overcome me. "Might I have a wee bite of something?"

Laughing at my request, Janis handed me a carrot.

"Ta, ta, love." I backed out the door munching my prize.

As I stepped outside, my busy mind reverted back to my earlier musings as though never interrupted. Slipping on my gloves as I stepped off the porch, I turned east and then walked briskly toward the lake. The air was cold and a stiff breeze blew across the ice-patched water. It was very quiet.

In 1938 everything had changed. It had been a year none of us would ever forget; especially that summer-a summer that had dragged on for an eternity.

"Getting a little poetic, Patrick Overly." I had spoken aloud and my own voice startled me as it drilled a small hole into the wall of silence that had settled over me. I found myself standing by the trees I had planted over the burned out ruins of a cabin, and the grave of a small white cat. I must remember to move the body before construction begins on the new addition, I thought.

"Quite right." I spoke to a blue jay overhead that seemed to be chastising me for forgetting such an important thing as the grave of Marshmallow.

I walked on; moving slowly; I admired the four new cottages, recently built. Lights were on in the three cabins occupied by staff; our gardeners, Washington and Sue Foster, our groundskeeper, Kendall Wiles, and our mechanic, Ian Reilly. Only Janis Jacoby's was dark.

I turned west, following the edge of the deck. I stopped again.

I suddenly felt very tired. I sat down on the door stoop from the staff apartments and closed my eyes.

Like a silent movie in my head, I watched my brother fall under a motorcycle, get up, fall under a deluge of blows from an unseen source, get up and then fall again. I could not stop the tears. I searched my pockets for a handkerchief but there was none so I used my scarf.

My heart ached for the series of devastating blows John Holmes had been dealt, which had left him with a crippled right leg and partial-paralysis of his right arm. The long wooden walkway, with its railings and ramps at both ends, a quiet testimony to his reliance on a wheelchair for mobility.

As though that were not enough, more misfortune followed. Holmes lost his first fiancee in an act of violence, his homeland had suffered near annihilation by German bombers, and many of his English friends had been lost followed closely by the death of his father. John could not even go home for the funeral because of the savage war. I found myself praying.

As I prayed, my agitation gradually lessened, my heavy breathing eased, my tears stopped flowing, and I felt relief. Something touched my shoulder.

Startled but not afraid, I looked into the eyes of Kendall Wiles.

Neither of us spoke for something like ten or fifteen minutes. I did not look to see. A light snow was falling.

"When did it start snowing?"

"An hour ago, sir. You have been sitting here for half that." He cleared his throat. "Pardon the intrusion, Mr. Overly, but I was worried."

"What time is it?"

"It is now 4:30, sir."

"I can't believe it. I've been out here that long?" I shivered. "Now, I'm cold. I had not even noticed before."

Kendall laughed and shook a dark gray head, liberally sprinkled with snowflakes. He wore earmuffs.

I laughed at the rather silly looking puffs of black fuzz.

"I hate hats," he supplied.

"Are you going to clean the walkway? I'll help if I may?"

Together we cleared the snow from the walk that ran from the Johnson residence to the main house. Kendall spread sand along it to add traction.

Now I was really cold. "I need to get inside before my fingers and toes freeze and drop off."

I offered my hand. "Thank you, Kendall, for everything."

"Don't mention it, sir."

"See you at 6:00 o'clock?"

"You bet." He walked toward his new cabin but stopped. "Sir, I love my new house."

I nodded.

When I entered my front door, Carrie met me. She helped me remove my snow-covered gear and literally guided me to the drawing room fireplace. I was too cold to resist.

I soon found myself in a chair, wrapped in a blanket, sipping hot coffee.

The hall clock chimed.

"It's 5:15," I muttered. "I don't believe it!"

"Believe it, mister." Carrie put her arms around my neck. "I was about to send out the Saint Bernards, or in our case, the Irish Wolfhounds. How did you get so wet?"

"I helped Kendall clean off the walkway and the deck." I pulled her around onto my lap.

Somewhere around the fourth kiss, there was a tap on the door. A second later, three toddlers ran in, scrambling to climb on my lap.

Their mother quickly vacated and took Hannah Elisabeth from Irene, the stand-in-nanny.

The children had all napped, had their snack, and were cleaned up for company. I kissed them and found myself thanking God one more time for all the wonderful things he had supplied. As we sat there hugging, my thoughts returned to the subject of Holmes.

Yes, he was in a wheelchair, but he was alive. He had his Detective Agency and he loved his work. He had his wonderful wife, Samantha, and their baby was due in March. He was surrounded by people who loved him. I must have smiled or made a sound because Carrie squeezed my hand.

"All right, darling?"

"Of course. Just thinking what a lucky man I am to have such a family."

It was 5:30 when the doorbell sounded. I heard Irene's voice welcoming the Farmer family.

Hudson and Sanford slid from my lap and took off for the front entryway. Carrie followed them; I followed her, carrying Lori Marie.

We greeted Owen Addison Farmer, 48, and his sons, Olsen and Phillip. The three had rescued Samantha and Holmes from death in a swollen stream in February. Members of a gang the detective agency was investigating, had forced them off the road. They replaced our groom and stable boy, both having joined the armed services. We were very fond of the family.

As we shook hands and hung up jackets, the telephone rang. After a brief conversation, I replaced the receiver.

"Samantha would like some help bringing the wheelchair across the walkway," I explained.

"Let me go, sir," said Olsen.

The boy was a strong, husky lad, perfectly capable, and I could tell by his attitude that he really wanted to do this. I nodded. "All right, Olsen. Thank you"

"Be careful. The walk may be slippery."

"Yes ma'am."

I watched him disappear into the dining room which led to the gallery and then onto the deck.

With Phillip leading the way with a sack of gifts, we all walked into the drawing room. The twins helped the older boy put the presents under the Christmas tree.

"You didn't have to do that, Owen."

"I know that, sir. It was important to my boys you know. It's the first Christmas without their mother."

The big man stopped walking.

I waited patiently by his side.

"Sorry, Mr. Overly."

Lori Marie leaned toward him, reaching out her arms.

The burly but gentle black man took the young girl. She squeezed his neck tightly and planted a wet kiss on his cheek.

"Why thank you, young miss." He kissed her on her strawberry birthmark. "Now I will have good luck all day."

"Why?"

"Well, Lori Marie, my mammy told us youngins that a strawberry on your cheek was from the kiss of an angel and every time we kissed that spot, we gonna have good luck, too."

My daughter's face glowed with excitement. She wiggled out of his arms and raced off to tell her mother about the 'kiss of an angel' on her cheek.

"You made that up?" I asked.

"No sir, my mother told us that cause her mother had told her." Owen winked. "It does wonders for the one with the mark."

"I can see that, Owen. Shall we go in?"

*****

Olsen carefully crossed the walkway, testing it for slipperiness as he walked. He breathed deeply of the clean December air, tinged with the smell of wood fires and loving it.

He rang the doorbell.

Samantha opened the door. Olsen stepped in.

Holmes was struggling to put on his overcoat, looking somewhat frustrated.

"Let me help you with that, sir."

After putting the foot rests up, Olsen lifted the man to his feet.

Samantha finished putting the coat on her husband.

In a matter of minutes they were ready. Holmes was quiet. Samantha was quiet.

Olsen looked from one to the other.

No one said anything.

The eighteen-year-old crossed his arms and took a firm stance between the door and the chair. "Okay, tell Uncle Olsen all about it! Sir," he added.

The degree of maturity in the voice startled Holmes.

Samantha giggled.

"Olsen, please stop calling me, Sir!"

"Okay, fine! Tell me what is wrong, John Holmes Johnson. Until you do, I'm not moving."

Samantha mumbled, "Excuse me," and disappeared in the direction of the bedroom.

Olsen saw the tears in her eyes.

Holmes closed his eyes and sighed sadly. "I never realized how much I rely on Malcolm and others, Olsen. It has been difficult for Samantha. I am rather large for her to support, plus she is six months pregnant." He spread his hands to the degree possible. "I feel…like such a blasted burden. We gave up the idea of a bath. There was no way she could get me in and out of a tub."

Shaking his head knowingly, Olsen said, "Ah, yes that explains it."

Holmes looked puzzled.

Olsen winked at Samantha, who had reappeared a few feet behind the wheelchair. She grinned at him.

"I thought I smelled something, and it wasn't your wife." The boy made a face. "Tis a pity."

John Holmes laughed.

Olsen laughed.

Samantha hugged her husband from behind and sniffed. "You are correct, Olsen. I accidentally spilled after-shave all over John's shirt. Maybe we should change it?"

By now, Holmes and Olsen were bent over, unable to stop their outburst of laughter. Samantha was drawn into it.

At last they were able to regain control just as Samantha answered the call of the doorbell.

Phillip stood there, hat in hand. "Need help?" he asked shyly.

"Get in here, little brother, and help me."

The three went down the hall to the bedroom, returning twenty minutes later.

"Much better, darling." She kissed him.

"Let's go then, I am hungry."

By the time the four had reached the house, the agency staff had arrived. The drawing room was overflowing with guests. For fifteen minutes, the friends all greeted each other and chatted merrily. William and Mollie Leonard had their triplets and, of course, their indispensable nanny, Veda Grantham. Her grandson, George St. Giles, greeted his fellow Englishman.

The Martin brothers shook John Holmes' hand. Isaac's wife, Samantha Jewell, kissed his cheek and Zeke's fiancee, Julia, copied her. The two women were secretaries at the office.

Also present was the rest of the Overly staff, the Fosters, Ian Reilly and Kendall Wiles. Ian was the mechanic and maintenance person. He could fix anything. The Fosters, Sue and Washington, were the gardeners.

"Let's go to dinner, shall we?" I took my wife's hand and led the way. Our twins were hopping and jumping in front of us.

It was a splendid meal. Under each plate I had placed a twenty-five dollar war bond. Imagine the surprise when we discovered one under every Overly plate, a surprise from my brother.

He raised an eyebrow at me in a truly comical manner and laughter sprang up like flowers on early-blooming fruit trees.

By 8:30 we were all settled in the drawing room around the Christmas tree, opening gifts. They were not fancy nor expensive but meaningful in their simplicity. Most of the gifts were handmade by the giver, relish from Veda, embroidered tea towels from Samantha Jewell, candy from Julia, hand-carved letter openers from Owen, and metal boot scrapers from his sons. From my staff each family received poinsettias from the greenhouse, coupons to be exchanged for special chores from Ian, and hand-made candles from Kendall.

"You made these, Kendall?" asked Carrie.

"Yes, ma'am. It's a hobby of mine."

"Excellent," said my brother. He sniffed the beautiful blue candle his wife had unwrapped. "Blueberry."

Everyone chuckled at the way he pronounced the word, more like blue-bur're. Most Americans would say blue-bear're.

I for one was very happy John Holmes had not forsaken his English accent despite his years in America.

The last gifts to be opened were from Zeke Martin. Everyone received a framed watercolor painting of their birthday flower, which would soon find a home in kitchen or bedroom. Even the children got paintings. Lori and Hannah had kittens in a flowerbed, Hudson, a jungle scene, Sanford's was a scene of the white cliffs of Dover, and the Farmer boys got paintings of their Labradors, Suki and Spencer.

George received a scene of Oxfordshire, England, his birthplace.

The last gift seemed to have been delivered and everyone was happy and content.

George carried his painting over to show it to John Holmes. They admired it together, pointing out places they recognized. "Let me see your painting, boss."

A strained silence stretched across the room, taut as a rubber band. Everyone suddenly realized that the Johnson's had been the only ones not receiving a painting.

I made eye contact with Zeke and left the room.

Isaac looked at his brother in shock.

Zeke winked at his younger sibling.

"Oh yes. My apologies, Holmes." Zeke spread his hands in an apologetic gesture and shrugged.

Holmes graciously nodded his way. "No problem, Zeke. After all, you did draw up our plans for our new house. I have no complaint."

"Do you mean that you don't want this, John Holmes? I would be happy to hang it in my home." I walked into the room with the large flat package draped in red cloth. I stood it up across from my brother and carefully removed the wrapping.

There was a soft chorus of appreciative comments as everyone admired the gorgeous 36"x48" oil painting.

Samantha knew by her husband's response to the gift that it was something very special. He was overcome by emotion. She hugged his head to her body, looking to me for an explanation.

I cleared my throat nervously. Speaking in a subdued tone, I explained. "I described the South Downs of Sussex to Zeke and shared photographs. This is the result."

"It's wonderful," Samantha said softly.

Even I could not take my eyes from the beauty of the painting. It was evening. The sky was darkening, tinged with pinks and oranges above the English Channel. The curve of the cliffs revealed the chalk limestone and the green rolling hills were dotted with the white specks of sheep. There were occasional stands of trees on hills and valley floors. A small group of buildings to the left represented the retirement estate of Sherlock Holmes where John Holmes had grown up: far to the right, a small cluster of lights revealed the presence of the Village of Fulworth. It was so real that I could smell the water and hear the waves lap the beach. My tears joined those of my brother's.

Neither of us could prevent it. Both of these places so loved by Holmes and so often visited by my family, had ceased to exist. They had been obliterated by Hitler's bombs and were no more.

Zeke Martin was embarrassed and sat with his head down.

No one knew what to do.

Fifteen minutes seemed to lumber reluctantly by as though dragged, kicking and screaming by the heels.

Hannah Elisabeth began to fuss. Carrie freed herself from my arms and picked up her daughter.

Zeke stood up and recovered the painting. "I am so sorry, Holmes. I didn't intend to hurt you so much."

Samantha pushed the wheelchair over to the distressed young man.

Holmes tried to stand up. Owen Farmer stepped forward and assisted him.

John Holmes touched the sad detective/artist on the shoulder. Zeke looked up into the gray, teary eyes of the Englishman.

In a slightly shaky voice, Holmes said, "I love it, Zeke. It is the most wonderful painting I have ever seen in my life. It is my home! I can hear the birds, see the flowers, and imagine walking the beach with my father. How can I thank you for that?" He choked up and had to stop.

The Englishman hugged the American and for a euphoric moment, there were no dry eyes save those of the sleeping triplets.

At a sudden loud cough by George St. Giles, the triplets began to cry. Hannah joined the trio.

The somber room exploded in bedlam.

"Oh my," said Mollie.

"Mercy," said Veda.

Hudson and Sanford covered their ears.

"Excuse us?" Carrie took her daughter out. Mollie, Veda, and Julia followed with the triplets.

"Indeed so, quite right. What a racket." Holmes reached toward Owen. Seated again, he addressed Zeke. "Please remove the cover, Zeke. I want to look at it. I want to drink it in."

Sanford climbed onto his uncle's lap. "What is that, uncle?"

"That is England, Sanford, my England."

Sunday was quiet and peaceful.

Monday was as unpredictable as the weather in the two Kansas Cities.

*****

As the Farmer family prepared to leave the party, John Holmes asked Olsen if he would be willing to spend the night at the residence. Olsen agreed.

This arrangement greatly reduced the burden on Samantha and she was pleased at her husband's thoughtfulness.

Monday, the boy was invited to go into Westport to spend the day at the Detective Agency if his father could spare him.

Samantha stopped the car at the stable. After a brief conversation, Owen approved the plan.

At Phillip's disappointed look, Holmes added, "Tomorrow will be Phillip's turn, that is, if he is interested in coming?" He looked at the young man, one eyebrow raised.

"Do I want to? Yes sir. Thank you, sir."

"Phillip, please!"

"Thank you, Holmes."

"That is much better. Tomorrow at 8:45, Phillip."

*****

Office business was proceeding quietly. Olsen was kept engaged in various jobs, even answering the telephone in the absence of both secretaries.

Jewell and Isaac Martin had gone to Defiance, Ohio to

spend three days with her family clan. Zeke Martin had driven his fiancee, Julia Harrison, and younger sister, Barbie, to Des Moines, Iowa to spend a day with their family.

There were only five in the office, including Olsen. It was a low-key day and they planned to close early. George went home with William for dinner. It was a chance for a good meal superior to his own cooking, an opportunity to play with the triplets, and to visit with his grandmother.

At 2:00 o'clock, Samantha came to the door of her husband's office. He was dictating information from his notes about their newest case. It was a slow job but Holmes was patient with the boy's efforts to keep up. It made Olsen feel like he was really participating.

"It is time to go, darling. I called the airport. The plane is expected at 2:45."

"Right. Let's put this away for now, Olsen, and go pick up my friend from New York. Have you met Francois?"

"I don't think so, sir, Holmes." Olsen grinned sheepishly.

Samantha chuckled as she helped her husband straighten up his desk. He liked everything in neat stacks and a clean sheet on the desk pad. The one new addition, just for the holidays, was the beautiful poinsettia plant from the Overly greenhouse.

"Come, Sir Holmes!"

Olsen laughed.

"Now don't start that, Samantha. 'Boss' is bad enough!"

"Quite right, my love." She kissed him while Olsen got the two matching gray herringbone overcoats from the clothes tree. He helped them.

*****

The three waited impatiently for the arrival of the Frenchman they had first met in May while investigating the death of Jean-

Jacques Henri Denis, cousin to Francois Jules Denis. They had become good friends. The man had hosted their visit to New York City just five months ago.

At last they saw him headed their way.

Francois waved and walked a little faster, closing the distance rapidly.

"Help me up, please."

When the two men met, Holmes was standing on his feet.

Francois hugged his friend and did two quick, almost kisses on his friend's cheeks, not wishing to embarrass the man. "Bon jour, mon ami. I am so happy to see you. You look well."

"And I you, Francois. Much has happened since we left you in September."

"And how are you, Samantha? You look wonderful."

They hugged and she kissed the man's cheek.

"All is well, Francois."

"Please meet our young friend. Olsen Farmer, meet Francois Jules Denis from Brooklyn Heights, New York. He is a friend of two of my friends, both are doctors, Doctors Fredrickson and Everett. How are they, my friend?"

"Doing well, Holmes." the Frenchman winked. "The Big E is now engaged to the Big J."

"Really! How exquisite."

Samantha laughed at their grins.

"And that's not all! Frederick is dating Janet's sister, Helen. Long distance, of course. It is amazing how many reasons the two men have for a trip to Kansas City." He sighed. "I am delighted."

Francois reached for his suitcase.

"Let me, sir."

"Thank you, Olsen."

Francois pushed the wheelchair following Samantha who walked beside Olsen.

Everyone at the estate eagerly awaited the arrival. Dinner was ready.

The black Ford pulled into the driveway at 4:10.

It was an excellent evening. The only other guest was Pastor Stephens.

Olsen went back to his cottage to have supper with his father and brother but returned when called to spend the night in the residence.

Francois stayed in a guestroom in the main house.

Malcolm and Marian were expected back Tuesday.

In the early morning of Tuesday the 29th, Sandra Rose Grun disappeared from her home.

An innocent tool
For refining and smoothing
Removing the flaws that mar
Or testing a man's patience-
Now a blood-stained clue

Chapter three

Metal Rods and Sandpaper
December 26, 1942

Detective Edwin Wylie Vernon with his young partner, Lee Emerson, drove up the long driveway to Judge Greene's beautiful home.

"Wow! Will you look at this place?" Lee whistled between his teeth. "This is as big as my Grandpa Fred's chicken farm and its right here in the heart of a city."

"Makes my place look like a doll house, kind of like the one my daughter, Mandy, got for Christmas."

"I understand developers have been trying to buy some of this land for several years."

"True, Lee. The Mission Hills area needs more room to expand.

Right now, that area butts right up to the Greene property. Very expensive houses on large lots. Most have carriage houses, triple garages, manicured lawns, wrought iron fences, swimming pools…"

"Stop, I get the picture."

Edwin parked the car in front of the colonnaded porch and got out.

An elderly man in a black suit stepped forward.

Showing the man his badge, Detective Vernon identified himself and then introduced his partner.

"Tyrone Wells, Detective." He offered his hand. "The family is waiting for you."

They followed him inside and then down a long wide corridor to a huge archway adorned with a garland of Christmas greenery. It smelled wonderful.

They walked in. The ivory carpet was thick and plush. The room smelled of pine and cinnamon. An ornate fireplace was busy about its business and a giant Christmas tree occupied one whole corner of the vast room.

Tyrone walked straight to the woman on the sofa. A walker stood beside her. A second sofa was occupied by a couple with two young children, all looking quite miserable.

The two detectives gathered in all these impressions in the seconds that it had taken them to walk the few feet from door to couch.

Lee noticed the view outside the window, the Renaissance paintings on the walls, and the wonderfully crafted hobbyhorse, now abandoned by its young owner.

"Detective Edwin Vernon, Madame. This is Detective Lee Emerson. Mrs. Greene, gentlemen."

Mrs. Greene offered her hand.

Edwin shook it. It was a firm, no-nonsense handshake. About six feet tall, he thought, she had been an athlete before the accident. He had read all about it in the newspaper. "Mrs. Greene."

Lee copied Edwin's action.

The silver head nodded and the green eyes were full of life, only slightly dimmed by the sadness of the moment.

"My eldest son, Kenneth, Detectives. His wife, Kathleen."

Kenneth introduced his children.

Introductions over, the detectives sat.

Mrs. Greene sent Tyrone for coffee and petite sandwiches.

Carolyn Wells, wife of Tyrone, came into the room accompanied by Wanda Rae Uland. The two women gently took the weeping children out of the room.

Edwin accepted coffee from Tyrone. "Thank you. We will need to speak to the person that found the body. I understand that it was your son."

"Yes, sir. He is in the kitchen. I will send him over." When everyone was served, he bustled out.

No one broke the silence as each took a first sip of the aromatic brew.

Lee tipped his cup toward Mrs. Greene. "Delicious, Madame."

"Thank you. It is a blend of two popular brands. It makes an unbeatable cup…" she faltered.

"It was my father's idea of a terrific cup of java."

Five minutes passed.

Edwin stood up. "We need to see the greenhouse. If you will excuse us, Mrs. Greene?"

"Of course." Kenneth stood.

A young man appeared in the door. "Seadon Wells, sir. You need to see me?"

"Walk with us, Seadon." Edwin turned back to Kenneth. "We will talk to each of you and eventually, to all of the staff, unless of course, your father died of natural causes such as a heart attack."

Genevieve stared through the huge window at the three

men talking on the wide porch, her eyes glistening with barely suppressed tears.

"Your father sent you to the greenhouse at 1:25 to announce lunch?"

"Yes. He was dead. I ran back inside and told the family. It was 1:30 by the mantle clock."

"Seadon, I want you to sit right here until we return from the greenhouse." He led the dazed man to the porch glider.

"Yes, sir."

"It is a wee nippy out here, Edwin," observed Lee Emerson.

Edwin seemed to realize that fact for the first time. "You are right, Lee. Second thought, Seadon, wait for us in the kitchen."

The young man walked toward the door.

"The greenhouse is open all the time?"

He turned to face the detective. "Why, no sir. The Judge kept it locked. It was his personal space. I used my key."

"Thank you."

At the door of the greenhouse the detectives hesitated, looking all around them. They entered, careful not to touch anything.

"Greetings, Doc. Any good news for me?"

"Afraid not, Detective."

Doc Hiram 'Socrates' Graham got up from his kneeling position next to the body. "The judge was murdered. The back of his head was caved in by one massive blow. A metal pipe right beside the body is the probable murder weapon." The doctor chuckled. "Good luck on this one, Edwin. Judge Greene was a popular and well-known figure in Kansas."

"Gee, thanks."

The doctor removed a rubber glove and they shook. "His watch was broken. It says 12:00 o'clock."

The body lay face down with head toward the south end of

the glass enclosed greenhouse. Edwin and Lee examined the area, made sure plenty of photographs were taken, and looked for signs of an intruder. The lab boys dusted for fingerprints and then prepared to leave. The metal pipe was bagged and placed in the lab van. The body was carried out.

Under the dead man's right cheek, in a pool of blood, Lee spotted a sheet of sandpaper. He stared at it for a moment, which drew his partner's attention.

"What is that?" asked Edwin.

"Sandpaper."

"Huh. Better bag it, boys." Edwin shrugged.

The two partners were alone.

"Hot in here."

"Indeed it is." Edwin laughed at himself. "I sound like that Englishman my brother talks about."

Lee laughed. He continued to walk around the greenhouse. "No windows, one door, locked by Seadon's testimony, no loose panels or holes in the walls, no secret entrances.

"Nope, not even an opening in the roof. And no footprints despite the wet walkway in here." Edwin Vernon scratched his head. "Well, it's a sure bet that the man did not hit himself on the back of the head. There is an answer here somewhere."

"Wonder what this rope is for?" Lee stood at the far north end of the round hothouse. A rope dangled from a wooden arm protruding out toward the center from a seven-foot post. A similar post stood at the south end. There were pulleys on each post.

"I have no clue. Let's go inside and talk to Seadon Wells."

Once outside, the men both shivered as the December cold contrasted with the heat of the greenhouse. Detective Vernon relocked the door and pocketed the key.

Lee stretched the yellow police tape across the door.

The two walked all around the building. Nothing appeared to be disturbed.

They went inside the mansion.

*****

At 2:45 Samantha parked in front of the two story wooden frame house at 52nd and Sunset Drive. The house was painted a pale shade of green while the gingerbread pattern of the trim was several complimentary shades of green and brown. It was very attractive. Samantha took a picture before getting the wheelchair out of the trunk.

A slim young woman with dark hair, long but up in a neat French roll, came out to the car. Without comment, she assisted in the transference of Holmes from car to chair.

The interior was attractively furnished with various setups of pottery arranged artistically. Original paintings adorned the walls. One room they passed on the way to the living room was clearly the workspace of an artist.

"You have an attractive collection of ceramics, Mrs. Grun."

"Please call me Sandra Rose, Mr. Johnson." She handed him a cup of coffee.

Samantha intercepted it and sat it on a small table to his left. She moved the chair to make it accessible to her husband.

"I'm sorry. I did not realize…"

"Quite all right, Sandra Rose."

"You are an artist? Do you sell your work?" Samantha was excited.

Sandra Rose crossed her long legs and laughed. "Yes to both questions. I teach painting at the Art Institute and what artist does not like his or her work purchased and on display in someone's home. Perhaps you are interested?"

"I am interested. I like your work. We are building a new home. Construction begins in the spring."

"Yes, I know that."

Death in a Green House

"Tell me how you know that and why you called us."

"Of course." She sat her cup down. "My husband worked for the JB Hobert Construction Company, Mr. Johnson. Eric spent twelve weeks at the Overly estate with a crew of nine, building four large cabins. The estate is the joint property of Patrick Overly and you, his foster brother, but he was born in England. You and Samantha live in a residence behind and west of the main house. You have two Scottish servants."

Holmes laughed then. "You are well informed. However, Malcolm and Marian Macdougal are employees, friends, and associates, rather than servants."

"Of course. The man is a detective with your agency. My husband..." she put her hand to her forehead for a second before continuing, "Eric was a friendly and likable man. He had the knack of easy banter. He could talk to anyone. He was an artist in his own way and was very perceptive."

She offered coffee to her guests and then refilled her own cup.

"I called your agency, Mr. Johnson, because it is my belief that Eric was murdered. It was made to look like suicide but I know better." She sat the cup down hard. Coffee sloshed out. Speaking as she wiped up the spill, she said, "I want to hire you, sir."

"Call me Holmes, Sandra Rose."

"Yes. Holmes." She handed an envelope to Samantha. "A retainer. I believe that is how it is done?" She folded her arms. "Three fifty from me, three fifty from my in-laws, Mary and Heinrich Grun."

"You would like two receipts?"

"Yes, please."

"All right, Sandra Rose, tell us about it. If the police are convinced it was suicide, why do you disagree?"

Her intense brown eyes bored into his sharp gray eyes.

She shifted her look to Samantha. "I knew my husband. Do you understand?"

Samantha returned the look and an unspoken alliance was formed. "I do," she said.

They left the attractive green house at 4:00 o'clock.

"Dinner is at 6:00, love."

"Quite right."

*****

Across town, Detective Joel Jacob Anderson of the Kansas City Missouri Police Department pulled up in front of a green stucco house at 75th and Grandview. Lab people were already at work and an ambulance pulled to the curb right behind his car.

It was 2:30 pm.

The two detectives went in the kitchen.

"Afternoon, Harris. What have we got here?"

James Harris stood up. "Lucille Lydia Sloan, 58, widow, lived alone. Her grandchildren found her, Joel. They are very upset. The son, daughter-in-law, and children are on the enclosed sun-porch, south end of the house."

"Death by metal bar?" Zeke pointed to the blood-covered rod on the floor.

"Yes, Zeke. Very observant, young fellow." The redheaded career policeman laughed softly, stifling his amusement, which seemed quite out of place in the presence of violent death.

"Any prints?"

"Several, from various places. I have a suspicion however, that they are all her prints." He shrugged. "We shall see."

The partners headed for the door as the ambulance men entered.

"We also found this under the body."

"What is it?"

"Sandpaper."

"Ugly scene."

"Quite right." Joel groaned at his own comment.

"Here is the sunroom."

As they entered the room, a thin man about 30 tried to get up from the sofa.

In a glance, Joel saw the braced legs, the pale face, and the terrified four-year-old clinging tenaciously to his father's neck. He stretched out his arm.

"Please, stay seated." He looked around the pleasant room full of plants.

Zeke brought two chairs and they sat down facing the family.

What a way to end the Christmas holiday, Joel was thinking.

Zeke took the initiative, introducing his senior partner, and then himself.

The man finally spoke, his voice trembling from the magnitude of their shaking experience.

"David Ault Sloan, Detectives, my wife, Charlotte, and our children. This is Daniel Dexter and Naomi Sue."

"I understand the children found…"

"My mother. Yes, sir. They ran ahead. I move rather slowly, polio when I was twelve."

Joel nodded. "My best friend is in a wheelchair." He blushed and looked at his hands. "I am sorry. That sounded very patronizing."

David actually smiled. "Think nothing of it, Detective Anderson. At least you did not yell at me as though I were ignorant, deaf and blind."

"Sir?" Zeke asked.

"Because of the braces," he patted his knee. Rude people will talk to me loudly as though I were deaf and address me in simplistic terms to make sure I understand. They treat me like I am retarded."

Zeke snorted. "That is ridiculous."

A policewoman entered the room.

"Mrs. Sloan, this is Officer Camp. Why don't you take the children upstairs while we talk to your husband? Try to help them relax, perhaps rest a bit yourself?"

Charlotte looked at David.

"Please." Joel offered his hand.

Agreeing with a nod, she gathered the fretting boy into her arms, and then she kissed her husband. The two women walked out together. The young girl had both her arms wrapped around the police officer for a measure of reassurance.

David closed his eyes and ran both hands through his thick wavy brown hair.

Joel waited.

"All right. What do you need to know?"

"Start with what time you arrived and go from there."

"We arrived at 1:25. The radio announcer said the time just as I turned off the car. I rang the bell three times. No answer. We went on in. She was expecting us," he explained.

"The door was unlocked?"

"No, sir. I used my key. As I picked up my sack of gifts," his voice broke, "the children ran ahead. They were so happy."

David Ault Sloan cried.

Hidden in the past
Old connections spring to view
Pulling like metallic threads
Separate and bizarre ties
Like a strong magnet

Chapter four

A Common Denominator
December 28 & 29, 1942

After a pleasant, relaxing Sunday, Monday proved to be stressful on both sides of the State Line.

While Detectives Vernon and Emerson interviewed family and staff at the Greene mansion, Detectives Anderson and Martin did the same at the Sloan home and neighborhood. The day was filled with information and notebooks overflowed.

In view of the fact that the greenhouse had been locked and only Seadon Wells had a key, on the surface he appeared a likely suspect. Also, for whatever reason, the Judge had strongly objected to the relationship between the gardener's son and the young maid. He threatened to fire the young man over the issue.

However, there had also been contention between father and son over the proposed sale of some of the Greene property. There was testimony from several sources, of heated arguments between the two men. Mrs. Greene had also had a voice in the disagreement as she was adamantly against selling any of the land. Judge Leroy Greene wanted to sell over half of the 340 acres and this had put a strain on their marriage.

And of course, there were the usual enemies a judge would make in the normal pursuit of his duties. Edwin Vernon had himself a mean case.

On the Sloan case, the son looked like a strong possibility as the murderer of his mother but Detective Joel Jacob Anderson did not think so. He was not at all sure, however. It was merely gut instinct.

The mother and son had been at odds with each other for several months over two volatile issues. One altercation involved the house. Legally the house belonged to David. His deceased father had left it to him with the stipulation that his mother could stay on as long as she desired to do so. David had allowed his mother to occupy the home, not really interested in living there in 1938. Times had changed.

The large house was far too much for the woman to handle alone, but she resisted his efforts, although she would agree that now, it would be a perfect fit for David, Charlotte, and their children. Nevertheless, the stubborn Lucille Lydia had blocked every effort by David to move in with his family. He had been trying for months to settle the dispute without resorting to forcibly taking possession.

The three adults had been very careful in their efforts to keep the children out of the disagreement.

The second argument concerned a lover. Lucille had been dating a younger man. That fact by itself was not so disagreeable, but he had been sleeping over, which David Ault strenuously opposed.

The detectives in both Kansas Cities, continued to dig deeper.

*****

That same Monday, John Holmes talked to Sandra Rose Grun on the telephone. Olsen Farmer and he went to the library to read newspaper clippings about Eric Fritz Grun's death. George St. Giles and Samantha Johnson went to Union Station at 2300 Main in Kansas City, Missouri. They examined the roof and the place where the fallen man had been found. They drove to the Hobert Construction Company office to interview Eric Grun's employer.

According to J.B. Hobert, owner of the company, Eric had been fired November 19 for anti-American acts and distributing Nazi literature.

J.B. introduced the detectives to his four sons, all employed by the company. After they talked to the four young men, the two detectives headed for the agency office. It was 12:45.

George drove. Samantha glanced over her notes.

"What did you think about his sons, George?"

"They were big."

She laughed. "Besides their size, I meant." She read from her notes. "Cal Brent Hobert, age 25. A tall 6'2," tan, muscular and a bit cocky. Lloyd Brock, age 24, tan, muscular and an insolent 6'2 ½". Faxon Brice, 23, tan, muscular, and defiant. Also 6'2 ½". And finally, Nevin Boyd, age 21, tan, muscular and hot-headed. Even he is an inch over 6'. The sons are all blonds. Unbelievably, they are all four bachelors." Samantha looked up as George parked the car. "Does that describe them?"

"Exactly."

"You are a man of few words, George."

"Sometimes." He got out and opened her door.

"You are right. This will wait until tomorrow."

Later that same day, Holmes, Samantha, and Olsen Farmer picked up Francois Jules Denis at the airport.

*****

Tuesday was very cold. This time, Phillip Farmer went to town with the detectives. Between 9:00 and 10:00 o'clock, Holmes tried five times to reach Sandra by telephone. The line was always busy.

At 10:15, Malcolm and Marian entered the office, back from their trip to Springfield, Missouri. The friends had coffee and chatted.

Holmes explained the new case.

At 11:15, the two women left to go to the estate; Samantha driving.

Malcolm drove Holmes to the Grun house with Phillip riding along.

"The green, green house, boss."

Phillip giggled.

"What, Malcolm?"

"Grun is green in German, callan. We are headed for the green, Green house."

At that moment, the radio announcer said the word, "Greene."

Malcolm turned up the volume.

"Judge Greene was found in his locked greenhouse, dead from a blow to the head. Detectives Vernon and Emerson are investigating. Across the state line, Detective Joel Anderson is investigating the murder of fifty-eight-year-old Lucille Lydia Sloan. She is the widow of John Clarence Sloan, a city housing Inspector for over thirty years. Mr. Sloan was killed four years ago in a car wreck. Here is an odd coincidence. Both victims live in green houses. That's the 11:00 o'clock news. Here is the weather report…"

The Scotsman turned off the radio. "Ye did say that Mrs. Grun lived in a green house, lad?"

"Quite right. Odd coincidence, wouldn't you say?"

"Aye. This is the causey, Holmes?"

"Yes. Second house on the right."

Malcolm got out and walked toward the house, then returned.

"What is it?"

"The front door is ajar, callan."

"Sorry, Phillip. Stay in the car."

Malcolm got Holmes out of the car and then lifted the wheelchair up the porch steps, backward. He positioned the chair to the left of the door and then he knocked. On his second knock the door swung open.

Malcolm slipped inside, gun drawn. He was back in less than three minutes. "Empty, lad."

"Take me in."

"Aye."

"Look for the phone. I called five times and got busy signals."

"She might have used the phone and then gone out, laddie."

"I know."

The telephone was on the bedroom floor. A coffee cup lay on its side, its contents spilled across the bedside table.

A framed photograph of Eric and Sandra Rose Grun was on the tiled floor of the kitchen, its glass broken.

The two stood stationary, looking all around the room.

Malcolm spotted small dark spots glistening on the tiled floor next to the kitchen table.

"Blude, ye think, callan?"

"Perhaps. You had better call the police."

"Aye."

He pushed the wheelchair out of the house, walked to the car and returned with Phillip. He went inside to make the call.

They waited on the front porch despite the chill.

*****

An hour and a half later, Malcolm wheeled Holmes into his office. He settled him at his desk.

"I wun gang tae Judy's for haggis, callan.

"How about roast beef sandwiches, instead, my friend."

Holmes laughed softly at the horrified expression on the face of Phillip Farmer at the mention of the Scottish dish.

"Aye," Malcolm said in a plaintive voice. "Com', laddie. I wud need ye're help."

George and Samantha had not returned yet so Holmes would be alone.

"I'm locking the yett, callan. I dinna want tae find ye missing when we return."

Holmes laughed at his friend, but at the same time, he was grateful. The last time he was alone in the suite of rooms their office occupied, kidnappers had just walked in and spirited him out and then down the back stairs.

Thinking about that experience brought his mind back to Sandra Rose. He prayed for her safety.

Shaking off the few seconds of lethargy, he picked up the telephone.

After two rings, a male voice with an ever so slight German accent, answered.

"Mr. Grun, this is John Holmes Johnson, Holmes Detective Agency. Your daughter-in-law hired us yesterday to look into the possibility that your son was murdered."

Holmes listened to the elderly man tell his wife who he was talking to on the telephone. His voice returned to the line.

"Thank you, Mr. Johnson. Thank you."

"Have either of you talked to Sandra Rose today, Mr. Grun?" He heard the man asking his wife.

"No, sir. What's wrong?" The words dripped with apprehension.

After explaining about the unanswered calls, the busy signals, and their visit to the house, Holmes finally said, "I believe she has been abducted."

Minutes later, he hung up the phone and sat staring out his window.

The telephone rang.

"Mr. Johnson, Detective Robert Wright, Kansas City, Missouri. I am at the Grun house to investigate Mrs. Grun's disappearance. I just spoke to a neighbor of the Grun's. He works nights and comes home at 2:30 a.m. He had just let himself into his house when he heard a car pull up outside. He said the engine made a distinctive pinging sound that seemed quite loud that early in the morning. He looked out and could just barely make out the shape of a car but it was in the shadows of several big trees."

"He couldn't identify make or color?"

"No, sir. The car was two houses down from the Grun residence. He did see two figures get out, definitely male he thought, judging from their size."

"Thank you, Detective. Not much to go on is there?"

"No, Mr. Johnson."

"Call me Holmes if you will."

"Thank you, Holmes. My name is Robert but I go by Bob." He paused as though thinking. "One more thing, its significance as yet unknown. Where the car was parked, we found an unused sheet of sandpaper."

"Sandpaper."

"Yes."

At 12:55, George and Samantha arrived. Five minutes later, Malcolm and Phillip walked in, laden down with a stupendous lunch.

Lounging around the conference table filled with a cold but varied assortment of eats, the relaxed group satisfied their hunger.

"Scrumptious, Malcolm. Ye out did yourself, mon."

"Why think ye kindly, lass."

"So, Phillip," asked Samantha, "how do you like detective work?"

"I think it's great. Maybe I can be an apprentice detective, when I'm out of school, of course. I have two more years."

"College, Phillip?"

"I don't think so, sir. College doesn't have as much appeal to me as it does to Olsen. I don't know, maybe trade school. Or, maybe I'll just stay a stable boy." He shrugged.

There was a contemplative silence.

*****

Detectives Edwin Vernon and Lee Emerson had spent hours Tuesday morning talking to employees at the Greene mansion.

In the afternoon, they looked through the Judge's office and desk, in downtown Kansas City, Kansas. Edwin talked to other judges in the courthouse. He interviewed office personnel, and the man's personal secretary, Elizabeth Hawn.

"Tell me about your boss, Mrs. Hawn."

"Leroy Eliott Greene was appointed a Criminal Court Judge in 1933 and has served in that capacity since. He had a reputation as an honest, fair man. He was thorough and conscientious."

"Did he have any cases involving Construction?"

"Yes. One case in particular stands out in my mind. In 1938 he presided over a case that involved illegal procedures and fraudulence claims in a Construction Company. They were building substandard buildings using inferior supplies, ignoring minimum standards required by law. The company was shut down."

Elizabeth toyed with her glasses a moment without continuing.

"What was the name of the company, Mrs. Hawn?" encouraged Edwin Vernon.

"I am sorry, Detective. It is hard to believe that he will not be walking through that door again. It was so sudden." She shuddered as though to bring her mind back to the man's questions.

"The name of the company was…Alexander Construction. It worked on both sides of State Line Road. A Housing Inspector named John Sloan investigated diligently on the case. He was later killed in a car accident, in November of that year. His truck veered off an icy road and smashed into a bridge abutment. He and Judge Greene had become very good friends."

"Will you provide me with names and addresses of other people who might wish harm on the judge because of his professional rulings? The principals in the Alexander firm, for example."

The woman did not answer.

"Mrs. Hawn?"

"Yes, of course. The owners of that particular company are long gone. Both died within a year of each other. Can you give me a little time?"

"Yes, ma'am. How about 4:00 this afternoon?" he stood up.

"That would be fine. Thank you."

"Either I or my partner, Detective Emerson, will stop by for it." He tipped his head her way and opened the door.

"Detective."

"Ma'am?"

"It was not Kenneth. I refuse to believe that his own son would bear that much ill-will against his father." She pursed her lips. "I don't believe it was Seadon Wells either." She suddenly laughed. "Of course, I am only a secretary and a friend of the family."

"I value your opinion, Mrs. Hawn. Thank you for sharing it."

He walked slowly to his car. His watch and his stomach said lunch time. He drove to a small restaurant where he had prearranged to meet his brother, Edgar, a Kansas City, Kansas lawyer for a hundred years.

Edwin laughed at his ridiculous thought. Edgar was the younger brother. There was a seven year difference in their ages, with two sisters between. Nevertheless, the brothers were very close and shared a special attachment.

Buttoning up his overcoat against the chill, Edwin walked quickly to Mazie's. His mouth watered at the thought of beef stroganoff and dark rye bread, two of his favorites.

"Greetings mighty warrior for peace and justice and the protection of the people." Herman Mazie pumped the hand of the detective.

Edwin had to laugh at the flowery language and theatrical flair of the restaurant owner. They had known each other for fourteen years. Both of them had twenty-one-year-old sons, who were also good friends.

"Your brother is here, my friend."

Edgar Vernon rose and greeted his sibling. "About time you got here. I was considering the appropriateness of eating the flowers." He motioned to the vase of fresh daisies on the table, a trademark of Mazie's

Edwin laughed as he removed his overcoat and hat.

He took his seat and opened the menu but he already knew what he wanted.

Their order given, the two sipped coffee a few minutes.

"Are you working the Judge Leroy Greene case, Edwin?"

He nodded and put his cup down. "Ever hear of the Alexander Construction Company?"

Their meals came and Edgar took several bites before answering.

"Yes, I have. It was a well-established firm in the area with a good reputation until the original owner died. Old man Alexander and his crew were hard workers and they did quality work. The firm passed to his two sons-in-law. Within ten years, their crooked schemes and shady practices brought the company down. It was sad to see."

"Ready for pie?"

"Indeed so."

Edwin laughed.

Edgar blushed.

"You've been talking to that English detective again?"

"This morning, as a matter of fact."

"What is he up to these days?"

"He and his wife are building a house and their baby is due in March.

He has a new case. A Mrs. Eric Grun hired him to prove that her husband did not commit suicide November 20 at Union Station. Heard of that?"

Edwin nodded, having just taken a large bite of pie.

"She thinks some of his fellow construction workers did him in. Now, she has disappeared."

The brothers finished their pie and poured more coffee.

"His friend in the Kansas City, Missouri Police Department, is working on the murder of Mrs. Lucille Lydia Sloan, widow of a building inspector killed in…" he stopped at the incredulous look on his brother's face. "What is it, Edwin?"

*****

In the office again, John Holmes was struggling to print the information he had received from Detective Wright, and also a note concerning his call to the Grun residence. He had made an appointment with the elderly couple for tomorrow at 10:00 o'clock.

"My therapy session is at 1:00 o'clock," he reminded himself, "then home for the New Year celebration."

He leaned back in his black leather chair and his thoughts turned to Sandra Rose. "Where are you, Sandra?"

A sudden noise from the outer office startled him. He dropped his pencil on the floor. "Blast it."

Phillip's head poked around the door. "I is sorry, massur."

John Holmes laughed and the young teenager grinned disarmingly.

"I am sorry, boss. I went for coffee for Malcolm and tripped over my own feet. I broke his cup." Phillip slipped inside and lowered his voice. "Think he will be mad?"

"No doubt about it. If I were you, I'd lay low until he calms down."

The boy's face clouded.

Holmes laughed again. "Sorry, Phillip. I was joking. There are extra cups underneath. Take him his coffee and come back if you will. I need your help."

"Yes, sir."

Holmes chuckled at the young boy's eagerness to please.

By 3:30, with Phillip's help, he had finished his notes and placed them in the appropriate file folder.

Samantha knocked on the door. She had a folder in her hand. She winked at her husband as she spoke to Phillip. "Malcolm wants you, if the boss is done with you."

"Yes, go right on, Phillip. Thank you for your help."

The boy left.

Samantha stood at the door, arms folded, looking at her husband.

"Come inside, Mrs. Johnson, and shut the door."

"Aye, callan."

She did as instructed. The folder went on the desk and she

leaned against his left shoulder. He put his arm behind her back.

"Give me a kiss?"

She rolled the chair back and sat down on his lap. After the third kiss, she pulled away.

"Enough, darling. We are at work."

"Oh, really."

Laughing, she removed his hand from her hip. "Really." She stood up and straightened her skirt. "My report about the Hobert Construction Company." She laid it open in front of him. "Ta ta, love."

Holmes had just finished reading about the four sons of J. B. Hobert, when the telephone demanded his attention.

"John Holmes Johnson. How may I help you?"

"Mr. Johnson. This is Detective Edwin Wylie Vernon. I believe you know my brother?"

By the time he hung up the telephone, John Holmes had a lot to think about.

Interesting when
Diverse points of view converge
Unique personalities
Unite to pool resources
Becoming allies

Chapter five

A Meeting of Minds
December 29 & 30, 1942

The Agency locked up at 4:30. Malcolm drove the couple home to the estate.

Francois Denis had come all the way from New York City for a visit and John Holmes was determined to put work out of mind for the evening. Always a tough assignment for my brother.

As a group, we talked and laughed. The three friends shared memories of the events in New York during their Honeymoon. They told us about meeting the Sherman family.

Francois shared the news with us, that Mr. Sherman, the elder, had died on the very day the American Navy had defeated the Japanese forces on Guadalcanal. His two grandsons were part of the marine forces on that battleground.

This information turned everyone's thoughts to the war. An uneasy silence stole across the room like a stage curtain.

Death in a Green House

Bustling noises came from the hallway.

"Oh, oh, here comes trouble. Brace yourselves," I said. My three toddlers burst through the open door in their pajamas to say goodnight. Their nanny was right behind them. Carrie came in carrying Hannah Elisabeth.

Everyone in the room received hugs and wet kisses.

Sanford stood at Francois Denis' knee, rubbing his left foot up and down the back of his right leg.

"What is it, Sanford?"

"Night, Uncle Franc. Would you like to see my room? I have flags from everywhere." Sanford spread his arms wide.

"And I have jungle animals," added Hudson.

"Come on." Sanford pulled on the man's arm.

Francois looked at his hosts with a nonverbal question.

"By all means, do go. The children are very proud of their rooms." I waved toward the door.

Francois stood up. "Well then, lead the way, mon ami."

Lori Maria slipped her hand into the Frenchman's.

"What do you have in your room, belle Lor-e?"

Lori giggled at the way he said her name. "I have a doll house. Want to see?"

"Oui, Mademoiselle."

The room seemed exceedingly quiet after the exuberant group left.

I saw John Holmes whisper something into his wife's ear; she nodded and kissed his forehead. His expression was somewhat wistful.

I made a mental note to myself to make an addition to our plans.

When Carrie returned, she squeezed my shoulders. I whispered into her ear, "Let's add an elevator so John Holmes can go upstairs."

My wife took my chin in her hands and planted a very big

treat before she settled down next to me on the large overstuffed sofa.

"Where is Francois?" asked Holmes.

Carrie chuckled before answering. "He is reading a bedtime story to the children and he seems to be enjoying himself immensely."

"Excellent."

The four of us sat peacefully content in the warmth and comfort given off from the blazing fire, the smell of apple and cinnamon, the fragrance of Christmas greenery, and the mellow glow of candle light.

At 9:25, Francois returned to take his place among us and all was well.

I played the piano softly; we sang a few songs and drank apple cider.

Francois sang, 'Silent Night' in French. It had never sounded more beautiful.

It was past midnight before we went to bed.

*****

John Holmes labored to crawl up the steep slope, trying desperately to reach the edge of a black hole. The ground was rocky and littered with broken glass shards. His hands and knees were hurting and his eyes were smarting from the cold, biting wind. He was shivering, yet his head burned as though feverish. At last, he pulled himself to the brink and reached for the hands of the figure hanging there, suspended in blackness. He grabbed a wrist with his hands but his right one had no strength. The body slipped from his grasp and fell. The anguished eyes of Sandra Rose Grun stared into his face. She screamed as she disappeared into the deep abyss.

For a moment there was only the sound of icy rain pelting the frozen ground all around him. His body began to slide. He plunged over the edge and hung there, upside down, suspended by his ankles for an eternity. His head was screaming in pain. A hand grabbed him from the depth of the chasm. He fell.

Holmes jerked violently. His eyes opened but only blackness surrounded him. A low, sustained moan escaped his lips. He became aware of the soft, sweet voice of his wife, crooning reassuringly.

Samantha cradled her husband's head and talked to him gently until he at last, began to relax.

"I'm sorry," he mumbled, his face buried in her nightgown. "I'm sorry."

"Better now, darling?"

"Yes, better now." He shuddered and lay back on his pillow, feeling spent.

Samantha lay by him, her head on his shoulder. "Want to tell me about the dream?"

He shook his head 'no' even as he spoke. "I saw Sandra Rose fall over a precipice and I could not save her."

There was a soft tap at the side door.

"Come in, Malcolm," said Samantha.

"Everything braw, lass? I thought I heard Holmes skreigh."

"He had a nightmare. I think he has gone back to sleep." She slipped out of the bed and padded silently into the bathroom where she vomited.

"I'll get Marian."

Marian came. She helped the shaken woman remove the soiled nightgown and put on a fresh one. The older woman led her to the bed and tucked her in.

Samantha cried silent tears.

Marian sat by the bed for the rest of the night.

At 6:00 o'clock, Marian returned to her apartment to dress.

Malcolm kissed his wife gently and sang 'Oh Danny Boy' softly, which helped her feel ready to face her day.

By 7:45, the four were at the breakfast table.

No one spoke of the dream.

The telephone rang at 8:00.

Holmes jumped involuntarily. "They have found Sandra Rose." He said it as a matter of fact.

Samantha took his right hand and kissed his fingers.

Malcolm left to take the call.

"And so the man took his concubine, and brought her forth unto them? And they knew her, and abused her all the night until the morning…" John Holmes stopped at his wife's sob. "I am afraid for her."

"I know, darling." She wiped her eyes. "Where is that unpleasant verse found?"

"Judges 19:25," he answered grimly.

A sober Malcolm Macdougal returned, standing statue-like in the doorway until his wife went into his arms.

"Ye were right, callan. They found Sandra Rose Grun in a shallow pit twenty miles west of Bonner Springs, Kansas."

"She is dead?" Samantha bit her lower lip as she waited for the answer.

"Na, lass, just alive. She is in vera bad condition. She has been to hell and back."

John Holmes closed his eyes. "Where did they take her?"

"Bethany Hospital." There was a long pause. The Scotsman sat down and stared at his breakfast. "The lass is with child."

The four finished breakfast mechanically and without tasting any of it.

At 10:00 o'clock, Samantha held the door while Malcolm pushed Holmes into the hospital. The elder Grun family would not be coming to his Agency office for their appointment.

George St. Giles met them in the lobby, escorting them to the waiting room. George and Samantha, entered. The others waited. Samantha came out with her arm around the shoulders of an elderly lady, and they walked away to find a ladies-room.

George held the door open for the wheelchair to pass. The tall, white-haired gentleman rose to meet them. He was slightly stooped in his posture. The left side of his face had a large scar and an indentation in the cheek.

He did not look steady on his feet.

"Please sit, Mr. Grun," said Holmes softly.

He stared at Holmes a moment, sighed, and then did as suggested.

George put a hand on the man's shoulder. "Mr. Grun, I would like you to meet John Holmes Johnson, my boss. Holmes, Mr. Heinrich Grun."

Holmes reached out with his left hand and the older man took it with both of his.

George introduced Malcolm.

No one spoke as they examined the terribly bruised young woman on the bed.

The old man began to speak. "I was born in Germany in 1879 but I never lived there. My father was an engineer. He built bridges and tunnels in a dozen countries. I speak six languages. I am an engineer, my son is in construction…was… was in construction." He shuddered. "I am sorry."

The man sighed heavily. "I fought in WWI against the country of my birth." His shaky hand went to his left cheek. "Shrapnel," he said. "Now the ugliness has overtaken Germany again." His brown eyes looked into John Holmes' before shifting to Malcolm's hazel eyes. "I am sincerely sorry about your homeland, gentlemen. If I were able, I would fight for the allies again, without hesitation."

Tension grew as the old man wiped his eyes and then buried his face in his large hands.

"She is pregnant with our first grandchild. If she dies…it is too early…we will lose them both."

"Mr. Grun?"

The man looked up just as the two women entered. Mary Grun went to the chair next to her husband; Samantha stood next to the wheelchair.

"This is Mr. Johnson, mother, and Mr. Macdougal. They are both from Great Britain." He kissed the delicate forehead tenderly.

"I am leaving George here as a guard just in case, Mr. Grun. We will take no chances that the perpetrators of this evil attack on Sandra Rose will not try to finish her off. I suspect they intended her to die in that hole, certainly not be found alive." He shifted his gaze to George. "We don't know the motive behind this yet."

"Understood, sir."

At 11:45 the three detectives set out to do lunch. Malcolm headed for Mazie's Restaurant in Kansas City, Kansas.

"Why are we going to this particular restaurant, boss?" asked his wife with an impish grin. "You have a falling out with your sister?"

Holmes chuckled despite the gloomy mood he was in. "Of course not. We are meeting Edgar Vernon and his brother, Edwin."

"Indeed, callan. Business or pleasure?"

"Both. Edwin Vernon is a detective for the Kansas City Kansas Police Department and our cases may overlap. Joel will be there also."

"My, my," said Samantha. "Should be interesting."

When the car arrived in the small parking lot, Joel was waiting. Together, he and Malcolm got the chair out and Holmes into it.

A short, squat man with giant laugh lines on his cherubic

Death in a Green House

face met them as they entered. He escorted them to a table. The Vernon brothers stood up as they approached.

"I am overwhelmed," said a happy Herman Mazie. "So many mighty warriors for peace and justice all at once. My head spins, my heart seems to pound..."

Edwin and Edgar Vernon both laughed at their friend.

"Enough, Herman. We are hungry. Preserving the peace is hard work," said Edwin.

"Yes, please do give us the menus," added his brother.

"Aye, aye, Mon Capitan." The intriguing little man greeted each of them in a different language as he handed over a menu with a flair. He was also very observant, because he had already realized that Holmes could not hold the large menu. He laid it open in front of the man.

"May I recommend the Yorkshire Pudding, Mr. Johnson? I have an English chef." He raised his eyebrows comically.

"Sounds wonderful. Yorkshire pudding it is. Thank you."

"You will want a pot of tea-Earl Grey, Darjeeling, or Keemun?"

"Keemun will be perfect, thank you."

"Very good sir." He wrote something on his pad. "You, Madame, might like the chicken cordon blue, and mint tea, perhaps?"

"That sounds delicious. I'll take it."

"Oui, Madame."

"Do ye by chance, have haggis, laddie?"

"Alas not. We are fresh out of sheep, sir."

Malcolm laughed heartily. "I'll take the Yorkshire and Earl Grey, thank ye, kindly"

Herman turned to Joel. "You, sir, are a burger and fries man. Am I right?"

Joel slapped his stomach jovially. "Bring it on Mr. Mazie."

"Please, call me Herman. Herman Mazie at your service."

"Stop showing off, Herman," said Edwin. "My usual, please." He winked.

"And you, sir?"

"What? You don't know what I want?"

Herman Mazie shrugged while a pained expression crossed his face. "Alas, who can read the muddled mind of a lawyer? Perhaps stew?"

"Why not?"

The man bustled off to submit their order and then he hurried to the door to greet more customers.

"He is wonderful. Where is he from?"

"No one knows, Samantha. He is an enigma to all who know him." Edwin picked up his glass of water and sipped slowly.

"So, what is this meeting all about?" asked Joel Anderson.

Edwin Vernon put his glass down and studied the detective a second before speaking.

Briefly and concisely he told the group about Judge Greene's murder, the Alexander Construction Company, and the dead housing inspector, John Sloan.

Their plates arrived. Herman stood by the table, ringing his hands while they took their first bites.

"Well?"

"Excellent, Herman."

All agreed.

The man hurried away.

"Ye think there be a connection between the cases?"

Edwin shrugged. "It is possible. Of course, we are shy of concrete facts but, yes, I believe there is a connection here." He finished the last bite of sourdough bread. "I find it hard to accept as coincidental that, one; a judge, who was a close friend of John Sloan, was killed. Two; who together closed a corrupt construction company, three; the man's widow was brutally slain, four; in your case, a construction worker is killed, then his wife was kidnapped, assaulted and left for dead, and six." He looked up at his captive audience; sandpaper at the site of each murder?"

"Just a wee streeked, dinna ye think?"

"Perhaps, but it won't hurt to consider the possibilities, will it?"

"Na, callan."

Edwin grinned. "Have I just been insulted?"

"Not at all, Edwin," said Holmes. "Callan just means young man."

"Well then, I take that as a compliment seeing as I am one year shy of the big five-o."

"Darling, you have eight minutes to get to your therapy session."

"Quite right."

"I'll get the tab, Holmes," said Edgar Vernon. "You owe me one."

"Indeed. A pleasure having lunch with you even if you are a lawyer. I am happy to meet you, Detective Vernon. Let us keep in touch and share anything that seems to support our theory. Agreed?"

"Agreed."

"Five minutes, callan."

"All right, all right. I'm coming." He sighed as he was whisked away.

Herman Mazie watched the hasty exit and then walked over to the table. He looked worried.

"They were unhappy with the food? Or the service? I talked too much?"

"Relax, Herman. They loved the food and I guarantee they will come back again. John Holmes had a one o'clock therapy session so they had to rush off. Relax," Edgar repeated.

"Very interesting colleagues you have, my friends. The man in the wheelchair, he will walk again, yes?"

The Vernon brothers looked at Joel for an answer.

"Circumstances are not in his favor but, knowing the stubborn tenacity of the man, I'd say yes to that question. He keeps getting knocked down but persistently gets up again." Joel shook his head affirmatively.

"I'd bet on it, that is, if I were a betting man," he hastily added.

Edwin Wylie finished his coffee and then got out his wallet. "I like you, Joel Anderson. Let me get your lunch. It will give us an excuse to meet for another, so you can repay me." He got out some bills and handed them to Herman.

Edgar did the same.

"You were correct, Edgar. These friends of yours are unique."

The three men stood up.

"Back to work," said Joel as he offered his hand.

"Quite right," said Edgar.

Edwin laughed and slapped his brother on the back as the three men moved toward the door.

The next time the brothers met, there would be no laughter.

Death pushes buttons
Starting a chain of events
That encompasses sorrow
Submerging people in pain
Struggling to cope

Chapter six

Families in Crisis
December 31, 1942-January 1,1943

Edwin read the information in front of him again, focusing on the names. An idea was percolating just beneath the surface of his conscious thought. He chewed on the inside of his right cheek, thinking. He read aloud, pulling the idea out into the open.

The librarian gave him a disapproving look. He ignored her.

"Alexander Construction was started in 1880 by two brothers, Thomas Aaron and James Erin Alexander. They developed a thriving business with a good reputation for fair, good quality work. James died in 1925 followed by his brother, Thomas, in 1928. The business passed on to the sons-in-law of Thomas. Robert B. Bartlett, husband of Cynthia Alexander, and Ted Thomas Horsley who had married Sylvia. Mrs. Bartlett left her husband in 1909 and has not been heard from since. Mrs.

Horsley died in childbirth in 1898, having had one son, Jabar Hobert Horsley."

Edwin tapped his fingers noiselessly on his knee. Jabar Hobert Horsely, he mused silently. "J.B. Hobert Construction?" he asked himself. Worth checking out, he thought. Even before the scandal, the son may have changed his name.

He returned to the article. "Mr. Bartlett died in 1938 before he could serve any time in jail. The business and all its assets were confiscated and sold to pay off debts and make some degree of reparation to the swindled customers. Mr. Horsely died in 1939 after serving only three months in prison."

Edwin refolded the 1940 newspaper. He glanced at his watch and stood up. "Time to pick up Lee and go to lunch."

He returned the stack of newspapers he had been studying, to the lady at the desk. Nodding his head at her, he started towards the door of the Kansas City Missouri Public Library. "Nice facility, ma'am."

"Thank you," she said crisply, not at all friendly.

Grinning impishly, Edwin Vernon stopped, turned around and then waved at her. "I'll be back," he said loudly.

A dozen heads snapped up all over the library.

Edwin chuckled as he stepped outside into the cold December wind. He wrapped the beautiful blue wool scarf his brother had given him for Christmas, tighter around his neck and walked briskly to his car.

At 2:35, he picked up his partner at the Kansas City, Kansas Library on Minnesota Avenue. They compared notes before Edwin drove the short distance to Mazie's restaurant.

Lee Emerson shook his head in agreement with the idea that a man with a name like that, might well have changed his name. "If my name was Jabar Hobert Horsely, I would change my name," he said emphatically. "Never mind the scandal created by your father being investigated and all."

Edwin started the car and backed out carefully. He drove

east two blocks and turned south on 5th Street. The streets seemed very quiet.

"Not many people out today."

"New Year's Eve, Lee. Let's head home after lunch. I would like to be with my family."

He sounded so wistful and melancholic that Lee glanced at his partner in surprise.

"What's wrong?"

Edwin shrugged. "I just suddenly want to see my wife and children. I don't know, Lee, it's just a vague feeling."

Edwin looked both ways on Ann Street before crossing it.

It happened so very fast.

From a parking lot to their left, a huge flat bed truck loaded with lumber poured into the street. It smashed into the driver's side and shoved the car into a retaining wall, crumpling car and men.

The truck backed up into the parking lot and sat there, leering at the chaos it had rendered. The driver was not visible even if there had been any witnesses to see him.

The ill-used truck pulled out of the lot, turned south and laboriously lumbered away.

Inside the smashed black Ford, dark red blood ran down Edwin Wylie Vernon's damaged face, soaking into the blue wool scarf. The silence was awful.

Lee Spillman Emerson listened to the silence, and cried because he could not move to help his friend.

A lumber truck, was his last thought.

*****

Edgar sipped coffee at Mazie's, wondering if Edwin would make it in today. I'll order if he is not here by 3:05, he told himself.

Herman Mazie approached him. "Telephone, my friend. At the counter."

"Thank you, Herman. Probably my brother saying he cannot make it here for lunch."

He walked to the phone casually, no hint or premonition of disaster on his mind, no bad omens or twinges of fright. In fact, he was in quite a good mood as he picked up the black instrument and lifted it to his ear. "Edgar here, is that you, Edwin?"

Edgar listened to the police officer tell him about the accident, not five blocks from where he stood. His face was as a white mask; his vision became suddenly blurred.

He sat down. But there was no stool or chair. He landed on the floor, dropping the telephone. Edgar Vernon passed out.

Herman raced to the side of his friend from his right, his son, Vaughn, hurried to the stricken man from behind the counter. They reached him at the same moment.

Herman loosed the man's tie and put a damp cloth on his head.

Vaughn Madison picked up the phone. He explained what had happened to the person on the line. The policeman repeated his message. Vaughn hung up.

Edgar woke up at 3:16. The big man was crying as the two men led him out of the establishment. They left their staff in charge while they took their friend to Bethany Hospital off Central Avenue.

In the waiting room, the three men were joined shortly by family of the two detectives.

Edgar struggled to his feet to greet his sister-in-law, Jodie Amelia and his ten-year-old niece, Mandy. He hugged them as they wept.

At 3:45, Ellery Vernon arrived from his job in Olathe; and his brother arrived ten minutes later. Curt Saxon and Ellery Alden, were Edwin's twins,by his first wife, Arlene. She had died when the boys were a mere six. Edwin had married Jodie in 1927. Mandy had been a surprise to the couple, born in 1932 when Edwin was 39, Jodie, 37. They were a very close family.

Edgar, a bachelor, embraced his brother's children with all the love he could tender. He was a wonderful, understanding, supportive uncle and all of the children reciprocated his love with their trust and affection.

The boys greeted him warmly. They shook and then hugged.

Lee Emerson's wife stepped through the door. Jodie instantly threw her arms around the younger woman. Celine Sarii Emerson was 36, three years younger than her husband. Their daughter, Lee Ann was only six. The couple had married in 1934, they daughter came in 1937.

While they waited in tense anxiety, two teams of doctors struggled valiantly to save the mangled detectives.

At 9:00 o'clock December 31, 1942, the families still waited for word.

Edgar sat cradling his niece in his arms. She had dozed off and her young face had relaxed. The man closed his eyes and he wished he knew how to pray. The only thing he could remember was the Lord's Prayer, so he repeated it, over and over again until, he too fell asleep.

At 7:00 A.M., New Year's Day, doctors reported that the men were in Intensive care, both alive but critical. No one could see them yet.

Edgar excused himself from the oppressive atmosphere of the waiting room. He hurried to the men's room where he was sick. After washing, he went to the nearest pay phone; he dialed John Holmes' residence.

"John Holmes Johnson. How may I help you?"

*****

John Holmes returned the phone to its cradle.

Samantha looked into his stricken face and knelt beside the man she loved. "What is it, darling?"

At 9:00 o'clock, Malcolm pushed Holmes into a waiting room full of worried people. Samantha came in right behind them.

Edgar rose to greet them. He made introductions.

A few minutes after 10:30, Joel Anderson arrived with Pastor Stephens. The families welcomed the pastor's offer to pray for their loved ones, and so he did.

The room was strangely silent for a good hour. Edgar Vernon and the four detectives, Samantha, Malcolm Joel, and John Holmes, huddled in a small compact group at one end, everyone else at the opposite end.

"It was a hit and run, Holmes, so the police say. They believe a large truck or piece of road equipment hit them broadside. They found yellow paint smears on the Ford." Edgar Vernon paused, wiping his weary eyes. "The police will investigate, I realize that, but..."

"But what, Edgar?" asked Holmes.

The man's strained brown eyes looked straight into the level gray ones of his friend. When he looked away, he found the hazel eyes of Malcolm Macdougal fixed on him. He opened his mouth but the words were hard to say.

"Aye, callan, we ken. Ye wad hae us look intae the drumbie."

"If you said, 'I want to hire your agency,' you are correct. If not?" Edgar shrugged. "I need to be involved, Holmes. I want to help my brother and his family." He touched the man's hand. "Please?"

"Of course. I want to help you, Edgar." He lifted his weak right hand and slid it on top of Edgar's. He squeezed.

The lawyer actually grinned. "Well done, Holmes. Your arm is recovering?"

"Quite right."

Their conversation stopped when the door opened.

Doctor Joseph Billings entered the room accompanied by a Doctor none of them knew; introduced him as Doctor Marris, the surgeon who had worked so long and hard to save the two men.

Doctor Marris addressed Mrs. Vernon. "Mrs. Vernon, you and your family may come to the room now, but only for a brief time. Everyone will have to leave then except you. There is a small settee in the room and we will put a cot in the room for you if you want to stay the night."

Around her soft sob, which was like a giant hiccup, Jodie Vernon managed to ask, "What about Lee? What about his partner?"

"It's all right. Mrs. Emerson can go to her husband, too. His injuries are only a little less serious than Edwin, since they were struck on the driver's side of the car and shoved into a wall."

Both women gasped.

"I am sorry. I should not have said that."

"It's all right, Doctor Marris. We need to know what happened. Please, may we go in now?"

"Yes, of course. Mrs. Emerson, this is Doctor Billings. He will take you to your husband's room. For the time being, they are in separate rooms."

The door closed behind them.

The room emptied considerably.

Joseph Billings returned and spoke to the group of detectives.

They all left at 12:45. After looking over the site of the wreck, the Scotsman, drove back to the Overly estate. There would be company arriving at 3:00 o'clock to celebrate the birthdays of Holmes and Patrick, born January first, one year apart..

It was a somber group, but determined to put aside sadness for the rest of that day.

Joel Anderson went home to collect his family for the party.

> Like an abacus
> Moving beads around to count
> The lives that become involved
> One by one by two by three
> Because of one man

Chapter seven

Extenuating Circumstances
January 1-7, 1943

The birthday celebration was quietly observed at the Overly Mansion with only family in attendance. The overall mood was pensive. Even the children were unusually silent before, and during dinner, as though they could comprehend the troubled state of the world right outside the walls of their respective homes.

In the two Kansas Cities, five families were equally pensive as they welcomed in the New Year without a loved one's presence. While the family of Judge Greene, and the family of Lucille Lydia Sloan, tried to make sense of their deaths, three other families kept vigil at the hospital beds of their injured family members.

*****

Neither Sandra Rose Grun, nor the detectives, Edgar Vernon and Lee Emerson, had regained consciousness. We prayed on their behalf.

Samantha was six months pregnant and not feeling well tonight. She sat listlessly on the sofa with her feet propped up on a footstool. Holmes sat close by her, staring into the fireplace.

And beyond the boundaries of the United States, war was raging on two fronts.

I listened to the clock tick as I examined each face in my large drawing room, and I made a decision. I whispered my idea to my wife and she rewarded me with a kiss.

Moving to the piano, I began to play a medley of tunes, making it up as I went along. I played, 'Sweet Irish Rose', and then 'When You Wore a Tulip', which faded into 'Farmer in the Dell', 'Three Blind Mice', and then 'Casey Junior'. Carrie sang alone for the first two, but gradually, one by one, the others joined her until all were singing with gusto. Before I could complete a number, someone would yell out a suggestion and we sang on and on.

At 8:30, I noticed that Hannah Elisabeth had gone to sleep on Aunt Samantha's burgeoning tummy; my young twins were yawning.

I played 'Happy Birthday' loudly.

Finally, I closed the piano and stood up, stretching and grinning at the beaming enthusiasm I had succeeded in generating. Even Samantha had joined in occasionally around the persistent, nagging cough that would not go away. I nodded at Davis. He rose to leave.

On his way out he tapped his twins on top their curly heads. Sean and Colin followed him out. When they returned, each held a box full of gifts.

Jenny entered with a huge cake and proceeded to light the candles.

There were seventeen, meant to abstractly represent our ages; John Holmes was 39 and I was 38. The children scrambled to line up, the oldest two holding the youngest two, and childish voices sang the 'Happy Birthday' ditty, breathlessly adding both our names at the end.

Joel took pictures. My brother and I blew out the candles; we opened gifts.

And so, our evening ended as merrily as one could hope for in a world so traumatized.

*****

Saturday, January 2, 1943, dawned with quiet dignity. Everyone slept just a tad later than normally and then proceeded to enjoy some personal solitude.

Gasoline had been rationed since December 1, so we all made an effort to conserve fuel as well as we could by eliminating extra trips into Kansas City. We also shared rides whenever possible. Sundays for example, we all squeezed into two cars instead of driving three.

Between phone calls from Kansas City, Holmes and Samantha worked on a jigsaw puzzle, one of three I had given my brother as a birthday present. The puzzles were scenes of London before the Blitz. This particular one was the beautiful St. Paul's Cathedral.

Midday Sunday, Holmes called the two hospitals to check on the condition of the injured detectives and Sandra Rose. There had been no change. All three were alive but still unconscious.

Lee Emerson would be the first of the three to awaken. The man opened his eyes on Monday the fourth but was unable to speak to anyone for another three days.

*****

"Come on in, Samantha," said Marta Cassiday. "Ron is almost ready for you."

Samantha smiled wanly and followed Marta into a treatment room.

The nurse and wife of Doctor Ron Cassiday helped Samantha into a gown. She took her temperature, her pulse and listened to her heartbeat. She felt her neck for swellings, checked her ears and throat, and finally, took a throat culture.

"What's wrong with me, Marta? I feel terrible." Samantha's eyes misted.

She coughed.

"Try to relax, darling. Ron will be in soon." She wrote on the chart and closed the folder. "Where is Holmes?"

Samantha looked away.

"You didn't tell him you were coming?"

She shook her head, no.

"Lie down."

When Samantha was horizontal on the examining table, Marta spread a sheet over her. She patted her hand reassuringly and left the room.

Taking a deep breath and letting it out fully, Samantha concentrated on relaxing her tense body. She rubbed her extended tummy and sang a soft lullaby, as though she could ease any apprehension her unborn son might be feeling.

She was dozing when Doctor Cassiday entered the small, but attractively decorated examining room. Marta slipped in behind him and shut the door. For a second they stood with arms around each other for a quick kiss and hug. Samantha was an old and dear friend, so that even should she awaken while they were embracing, it would not matter. She would understand.

In her uneasy sleep, Samantha heard the sound of a door, felt the touch of a hand, and imagined a brush of lips on hers.

She gripped the hand tightly and smiled in her sleep as she heard her name.

"Samantha."

Her eyes fluttered.

"Samantha, its Ron Cassidy. Wake up, please."

"Hello, Doctor Ron," she said sheepishly. "I fell asleep?"

"Indeed you did. That's all right. You need the rest. We need to talk, Samantha. Are you fully awake now?"

"Is something wrong?"

At 2:30, Ron Cassiday went into his office and dialed Myra Warner's Physical Therapy Clinic. He identified himself to the receptionist, and asked for Myra. Ron explained about Samantha's infection and the need for her to go straight home. Myra agreed to tell Holmes and have him come to Ron's office as soon as his therapy treatment was over. "Or should I interrupt it?" she asked.

"How much longer will it be?"

Glancing at her watch, Myra answered, "Twenty minutes, ten more to dress."

"That will be fine. She is resting on one of the tables and I have given her medication. I just don't want her driving herself home under these conditions." He paused. "Myra?"

"Yes?"

"Please reassure him that she is not seriously ill nor is the baby in any danger at this point."

"Got it. Nothing to worry about."

Myra Warner walked to treatment room three and knocked.

"Come in," said two masculine voices.

Harvey Williams was working on John Holmes' right arm when Myra entered. She pulled up a chair, and folded her arms nonchalantly.

"So, how was your birthday, John Holmes?"

Death in a Green House

"Great." He told her about the songfest, the gifts, and the cake.

"How was Samantha feeling?"

John Holmes' smile faded. "She wasn't feeling very good." He looked apprehensive. "Why do you ask?"

Good start, she chided herself.

"Relax, my friend." She took his left hand as she made eye contact with Harvey.

Nodding slightly, Harvey began his final rubdown.

"While you were here, Holmes, Samantha drove herself to Doctor Cassiday's office for a check up." She squeezed his hand. "It is nothing serious and the baby is in no danger. Let me finish before you get all upset and bothered, okay?"

He let out the breath he had been holding. "All right, Myra. Please continue."

"She has an infection, quite treatable, I assure you. He wants you to come over to his office when you leave here and see your wife home. He doesn't want her to drive herself because of the medication. Understand?"

"Quite." He rubbed his forehead.

"Okay, my man. You are finished. Go pick up that pretty wife of yours."

At 3:10, Malcolm wheeled Holmes into the Cassiday Clinic. He told the woman at the desk who they were. She showed them to the room where Samantha was sleeping.

Malcolm pushed the wheelchair near the table and Holmes took his wife's hand. The Scotsman started to leave.

"Stay, Malcolm. Please."

"Aye, callan. As ye wish."

Ron Cassiday entered. He actually hugged the chair-bound man. "It's about time you came to see me, old friend. I am delighted you have not needed my services, however." He shook hands with the big man standing behind the chair. "You and your wife are well?"

"Aye. Thank ye for caring."

Samantha woke up.

"Good, Sleeping Beauty is back with us."

Samantha managed a smile.

Ron settled back in the chair he had pulled up close to the table. "Okay, here is the bottom line. Your wife has pneumonia. She needs rest, relaxation, lots of fluids, medication, and no more working until after the baby is born. She needs to stay home, sleep a lot and plan the nursery. Doctor's orders."

The three detectives looked at him rather blankly.

"Questions?"

Holmes nodded his head and opened his mouth but nothing came out.

Ron's eyebrow went up.

Malcolm suddenly laughed. "He canna believe that the time is so nearhand. The callan is donnered."

Ronald Cassiday laughed with Malcolm.

Holmes looked dazed.

Samantha coughed.

*****

Tuesday morning, a stubborn Samantha Louise Johnson, insisted on joining her husband at the breakfast table. She sipped tea laced with honey while the others ate.

Once the two men had left the house, she needed no persuasion to return to bed. The simple act of walking to the bedroom sapped whatever energy she still had. Marian settled her comfortably and kissed her moist cheek.

Malcolm saw Holmes to his office, greeted the two secretaries, and left again. He drove to the hospital to relieve George St. Giles from guard duty. Sandra Rose was still unconscious.

So far there had been no attempts on her life, an encouraging sign.

At the office, Julia had just said good-bye to her fiancé, Detective Zeke Martin, and hung up the telephone as the boss had been wheeled in.

She greeted the two men cheerfully.

Samantha Jewell joined her soon to be, sister-in-law.

John Holmes Johnson returned the cheery, 'good morning' with a tentative smile. Malcolm settled him in his office and headed out.

As he left the office, Malcolm explained to the girls about Samantha's illness.

Julia took a phone call just as the front door closed behind the Scotsman. She wrote down the message and hung up.

With a cup of hot tea, two letters for signatures, and the message, Julia went to John Holmes' office. She rapped at the open door and then entered when he looked up at her.

He signed the letters and thanked her for the tea.

He was reading the message as she left the office.

"Julia?"

"Yes, boss."

He actually chuckled before he said, "When George arrives, I would like to speak to him."

"Right." She waited a second. "Anything else?"

Holmes tapped his fingers on the desk, shaking his head slowly. "No, not yet anyway. I've got to think." He waved his left hand around his head.

Julia laughed at the familiar gesture. "Everything will be okay, boss, trust me." She winked at him

Holmes waited impatiently for the 10:00 o'clock appointment. He read the message again. Reading it aloud, he pondered the note. "J.B. Hobert and son, Faxon, to see you at ten, if convenient." He drank his tea. "This should be interesting."

The two men arrived at 10:05. Julia showed them in, closing the door behind her as she left.

The Hobert men looked uncomfortable.

A minute passed. J.B. glanced around the office. Faxon stared at the window as though unwilling to make eye contact with the detective.

"Won't you sit down?" said Holmes softly. "How may I help you?"

The two at last took seats. Faxon fiddled with his hat. J.B. crossed his arms in a determined example of body language.

Holmes waited.

Another three minutes eked by before anyone spoke up.

"Mr. Johnson," said a determined man, " I have something to share with you, and then my son has an important piece of information to tell you." The man sighed heavily, and suddenly looked very tired. "My name was Jabar Hobert Horsley before I changed it. My father was Ted Thomas Horsley." He paused.

"I don't understand. Please continue."

"My father and his partner, Robert B. Bartlett, were the sons-in-law of Thomas Aaron Alexander of the Construction Company of the same name. They were the two men responsible for ruining the company. My father died in jail." He spread his hands in a helpless gesture. "It's only a matter of time before someone figures it out. Detective Edwin Vernon is sharp. He may have already discovered my relationship to the Alexander firm, which leads to my connection with Judge Greene, and in a roundabout way, John Sloan and his widow."

"Why are you telling me this?" He tapped his fingers on the desk.

"I'll get to that, Mr. Johnson. First, listen to my son. Faxon?"

Faxon Brice Hobert looked defiant for a second but wilted under the glare from his father's steady, strong eyes. The older man had strong patriarchal influence over his sons.

"I was Lucille Lydia Sloan's lover." He dropped his hat on the bench beside him and then put his head down, forehead in his hands. "We quarreled December 23 when I told her we were through, I had met another and wanted to marry." He lifted his head and made eye contact with Holmes. "I did not kill her, sir. Can you help me?"

"You expect to be accused so you want to hire the Agency?"

"Yes, sir."

Holmes stared at the opposite wall for a second, thinking. He unconsciously chewed on his lower lip as he considered the request. Finally, he looked up at the younger Hobert. "I will look into this for a few days before I officially accept. If I feel the evidence points to you, I will not suppress it, nor shield you from the police. Do you agree?"

"Yes," said J.B.

Faxon nodded. "Agreed."

"Have you heard about Detectives Vernon and Emerson?"

"They are investigating Judge Greene's murder."

"And a detective named Anderson is doing the same for poor Lucille," added Faxon.

"Quite right, however, at the moment, the two Kansas City, Kansas officers are fighting for their lives in Bethany Hospital. They were struck down by a large vehicle of some undetermined type."

Both men looked genuinely shocked at the revelation.

Holmes watched their eyes intently, observing their manner at the news and he felt certain that these two had had no previous knowledge of the accident. He did not think they had anything to do with it.

"I and another detective will come to your office tomorrow morning. We need to talk to all four of your sons. Is that acceptable? Let's say 9:30?"

"Of course."

"I will also like to talk to some of the employees that worked with Eric Fritz Grun. I am on that case also. Any objection?"

"No, sir. Eric was my friend." Faxon paused. "I do not believe he did any of those things, especially passing out those pamphlets, and I certainly don't think he committed suicide."

It was 11:45 before the two men left the Agency office.

Holmes sat with his eyes closed, thinking about the whole situation.

He reached for the telephone just as there was a rap on his door.

"Come." He dialed the hospital just as George St. Giles entered the room. He waved him to a seat.

After a five minute conversation, Holmes hung up.

"Lee Emerson woke up but is unable to talk yet. No change in Detective Vernon's condition."

"You have a job for me, boss?"

"Indeed."

George listened carefully to the newest pieces of information, jotting down some names in his ever-present notebook. His job was to do some research and confirm the facts given to the Agency by J.B. Hobert.

After the younger detective left the office, John Holmes called home.

The next day George St. Giles drove Holmes to the office of the Hobert Company. He drove west on highway 32.

"Where is this place, George?"

"Edwardsville, boss."

"Edwardsville?"

George chuckled. It is a dot on the roadmap, Holmes."

"I see."

It was a gray morning with a threat of snow. George pulled into a lot filled with a variety of construction vehicles. Following a sign, he parked in front of the small building that served as an office.

Faxon met them as George got out of the car. He helped with the wheelchair, pushing it into the warm office, still sporting its Christmas decorations.

J.B. Hobert greeted the two detectives and then introduced his other three sons to John Holmes.

Cal shook hands with both men. "We have met before," he said to George.

"Indeed. I was here December 28 with another detective, Samantha Johnson. Unfortunately, she is ill."

"I am sorry to hear it." Cal turned to Holmes. "She is your wife, Mr. Johnson?"

After his confirmation and murmured condolences, the introductions continued.

Lloyd shook with a slight sneer on his face. Eyeing George as they shook, he said insolently, "You his gofer?" He folded his arms and leaned back against the wall, glaring at John Holmes the while.

"Lloyd, behave yourself. I'll have none of that."

Glancing at his father, he nodded. He looked down at his boots as he said, "Sorry," with very little conviction.

George brushed his brown hair back from his face and grinned. "I'm not offended, Mr. Hobert. I don't know what it means."

Nevin stepped forward, laughing at his older brother's discomfort. Extending his hand, he supplied his name and age. "Nevin Boyd Hobert, 21. I'm the baby of the family. Gofer means he gives the orders, you do the running. Its connotation is meant to be uncomplimentary."

"Understood. Thank you for the explanation." George glanced at his boss. "Do I get a raise to go with my new title?"

"Afraid not, old chap. So sorry."

The younger Englishman made a face; Holmes laughed.

"Let's all sit, shall we?" J. B. led the way, sitting down behind his desk.

When all were settled, Lloyd spoke first. "You are both British?"

"Quite right, Lloyd. May we address you all by your first name?"

"Of course."

A thick silence imbibed the room.

J.B. moved and his chair squealed.

His sons looked at him as though trying to ascertain what this fuss was all about without actually asking. Another minute went by.

"I told Mr. Johnson about your grandfather. It would have come out eventually."

"Why?" asked Lloyd, with an angry tone to his voice.

"Because of the connection between grandpa's business, and Judge Greene. I told him about Lucille and I." Faxon shook his head, looking like a bear waking up from his long hibernation. "Sorry about this mess."

"That's all right," said Cal. "Things happen."

"It's not all right," yelled Nevin. He struck the desktop with his fist. The sound reiterated his hostility. "I don't get it. Why are we airing all this to two strangers?" He swept his arm toward the two men. "Why?"

"Shut up, Nevin." The elder man's tone was sharp.

Nevin jumped up from his seat. The chair fell backward with a loud crash.

"Sit down," said the oldest brother. Cal looked at his brother with an astonished expression. "Don't you get it? The police might think Faxon killed Lucille. She was the widow of the John Sloan who worked with the dead Judge to close grandfather's business. They might think pa killed the judge."

With a curse, Lloyd added, "They might even think one or more of us did one, two, or all three murders."

"Three, what three?"

Faxon answered Nevin's question. "The supposed suicide of my friend, Eric Grun. You are a suspect too, little brother. Better watch your temper."

"Yes, for heaven's sake, calm down."

"I didn't kill nobody." He sat down abruptly. "I don't believe any of this." Nevin actually looked at Holmes, full in the face. "You going to help us or not?"

Holmes nodded once. "Quite right."

"What do you need, Mr. Johnson?"

Holmes shifted his eyes back to J.B. Hobert. "Where, precisely each of you were as the following events were taking place. Witnesses to your presence there would help. Most importantly, I need the truth from you, gentlemen. Read them those dates if you will, George." Holmes laughed, "or should I say, Gofer?"

Lloyd actually laughed at the suggestion.

"I prefer George, boss." He opened his notebook. "Friday 11-20, Eric Grun's death. Saturday, 12-26 between 1 a.m. and 1:30 p.m. when Lucille Sloan was murdered, and Judge Greene was killed. Monday 12-28 between midnight and 3 a.m. when Sandra Rose Grun was kidnapped, and finally, Thursday 12-31 between 11 a.m. and 1 p.m. a large vehicle struck a police car injuring two Kansas City, Kansas officers."

"That's a tall order. We move around a lot in a job like this. We do have a record of jobs and who was on which." J.B. stood up. I'll get it for you."

Faxon coughed. "I was with Lucille the 26th until 11:45. We went out to dinner at the Italian Gardens on Main Street. After we ate, we went to her house.

I meant to stay the night." He looked down at his hands. "Instead, we quarreled and I left. No witnesses."

"Anyone know when Faxon got home on the 26th?"

"It was Saturday, man. We were all out. I took my girl to a movie."

"I'll need to speak to her."

"Is that necessary?"

"Yes, Nevin. I am sorry, but I must confirm your story."

He reluctantly gave the information to George.

There was a knock on the office door.

Joel Jacob Anderson sauntered in, followed by his partner, Zeke Martin.

"Hello, Holmes. Quite a surprise, meeting you here."

Holmes introduced the two Kansas City detectives to the Hoberts.

Pleasantries over, Joel turned his attention to Faxon Hobert. "Faxon Brice Hobert, I'm placing you under arrest for suspicion of murder. You need to come with us."

With a deep sigh of resignation, the man rose from his chair.

The youngest sibling leaped up with a cry of anguish and frustration. He shoved his brother back against the wall.

"No," he screamed, "you can't do this. No way."

Nevin Boyd looked ready to fight off the two detectives. His face turned red, his nostrils flared. The tension in the room was profound.

Faxon laid a hand on the young man's shoulder and called his name gently. "Nevin."

Their eyes met.

"This isn't helping me, Nevin. Do you understand? I have to go, don't you see that?"

With super swiftness, Nevin Boyd's angry outburst dissipated like sloughing off old skin. He hugged his brother. "I'm sorry. You didn't kill her." He looked into the man's face as he added, "Did you?"

"No, little brother."

Slapping his brother's back softly, he firmly pushed him

into Cal's arms, turned, and then he stepped toward Joel Anderson.

Joel got out his handcuffs; Faxon put his hands out.

"The best thing you can do for me, Nevin, is help Mr. Johnson."

A group of six watched soberly as the police car drove off the construction company lot.

The small porch was so full that not one more could have fit on it and Holmes could not turn his chair to face the Hobert's.

"If you boys will trust us, we will do all in our power to clear Faxon. Like you, I don't believe he did it. Is it a deal?"

"Deal," said J.B. He stepped back into the office.

One by one, the three sons followed their father inside and George wheeled Holmes in.

Some time later, George drove Holmes to his therapy session at Myra's Clinic. It was 1:05.

*****

It was Thursday January 7. In Kansas City, Kansas, Detective Charlie Skylar Raymond sat at his desk examining the folder marked Judge Leroy Greene. It was written in the odd, slightly scribbled handwriting of Edwin Vernon. When he came upon the neatly printed out, precisely spaced notes done by Lee Emerson, Charlie chuckled at the contrast.

He closed the file. He was not happy to have inherited such an important case in the manner in which the transference had occurred. The two injured detectives would not be out of the hospital for weeks; indeed, Edwin was not even out of danger of death yet. Lee was awake and responding to treatment. Charlie shook his head and crossed himself. He picked up the telephone.

Charlie Raymond was short. He measured 5'6 ½" in his

stocking feet. At 52, he was already bald on top of his head with a fringe of deep chocolate brown hair from ear to ear. He always looked rumpled, and tended to wear the same shirt far too long. A bachelor, he was a competent cook, which accounted for a leaning toward pudgy.

Despite any ribbing he took from his colleagues, Charlie was respected in the department. He was a smart man.

At 1:00 o'clock, he put on his trademark black hat that had long since lost all resemblance to the once attractive Stetson it had been when new. He left his office with a list of stops, which he posted in his usual way on the dash of his car, also, slightly rumpled in appearance.

"Item one: pick up partner," he read aloud. "Item two: stop at the hospital; item three: lunch at Italian Gardens?; item four: appointment with John Holmes Johnson at 4:30." He tapped the list with a stubby finger. "Who are you and what do you have to do with this case?" he asked aloud.

Parking in front of a small, modest house on 45th Street between Parallel and Leavenworth Road, Charlie went to the door and used the ornate doorknocker. His partner was very fond of the classic tale by Charles Dickens, 'A Christmas Carol'. He particularly liked the part about the doorknocker changing to the face of Jacob Marley. He bought his first one in 1930 and now had a collection of twelve.

Innes Mason Wallace came to the door. Charlie stepped inside.

Adrienne Gregory, named after her great grandfather, kissed Charlie on the cheek while her husband of thirty years donned his coat and scarf.

Once in the car and on their way, Innes automatically struck a line through the top item. "Item two: stop at hospital."

The car was quiet for half the distance between 45th and Parallel and Bethany Hospital off 10th and Central.

"Welcome to the New Year, Charlie."

"Thank you. Same to you, partner."

Charlie parked the car. He turned to look squarely into the face of his partner, his junior by two years. "I want to thank you, Innes."

"For what, Charlie?"

He stared at the steering wheel a second before answering. "For making me a part of your Christmas celebration for the last ten years. For putting up with my faults, not to mention my looks." He looked at his partner. "For being my partner for ten whole years, come January 10. You're the first you know…"

"To stick it out?" finished Innes. He shrugged, slightly embarrassed. "I like you, Charlie Raymond and you are welcome. Why so serious?"

They got out of the car. "Edwin and Lee, they've been partners for ten years also, April, I think."

"March."

"April," repeated Charlie as he held the door for his partner.

"March," said a stubborn Innes.

Charlie gave in first. He laughed. "March it is." He put his hand on his partner's shoulder, only 2" taller than himself. They walked almost shoulder to shoulder toward the room of Edwin Vernon.

*****

At the Detective Agency, Westport Road and Mill Street, John Holmes hung up the telephone after a brief conversation with a Detective Raymond. The conversation brought his mind back to the three people in the hospital. He dialed the phone. It was 10:50.

At the hospital, Malcolm Macdougal sat outside the room of Sandra Rose Grun, on guard duty. Holmes was concerned that the perpetrators of the attack on her would not want her talking to the police. He was unwilling to take a chance with her life.

Malcolm was bored. His watch said 10:50.

Detectives Raymond and Wallace walked down the corridor toward the Scotsman, looking at each room number.

Malcolm saw the two short, rather frumpy looking men making their way slowly toward him. He was instantly alert. He unbuttoned his coat to make his gun, if needed, easier to reach.

The approaching men stopped two doors down by a cross-hall, glancing around as though confused.

The taller of the two headed his way. He stood up.

About four feet away, Innes stopped. Something about the man's eyes and posture warned him to be cautious.

"Detective Innes Wallace, KCKPD. I'm looking for the room of Detective Vernon." He sensed, rather than saw, his partner move forward.

He raised his right hand slowly to stop him.

"Got an ID, laddie?" Malcolm had his hand on his gun, which was in plain view to both the other men.

Very carefully, Innes got out his badge. "Ease off."

"Put it doun and back awa."

"Aye." Innes backed up five paces.

Malcolm checked it carefully and then he grinned sheepishly. "Sary. Detective Malcolm Macdougal on guard duty here."

"May I see your ID?"

"Aye, callan, I dinna mean to make ye fash." He slid his license over to the man. "Private Investigator protecting an assault victim."

Innes signaled his partner. The three introduced themselves more thoroughly.

"So you work for the Holmes Detective Agency. I have an appointment with the head man at 4:30 today," offered Charlie. "Any idea why his name is in Detective Vernon's report?"

"Indeed so. Edwin Vernon thinks our cases are related somehow. The mon is in the second room, left side, down that corridor ye just passed."

The two turned to leave.

"Innes Wallace is a fine Scottish name, lad. Were ye born in Scotland?"

"Aye, I was indeed. Falkland in Fife. But alace, we moved to the United States when I was a wee lad. I've nearly lost all trace of my brogue."

The 6'4" man shook hands with the two shorter men. "Ye wad be wise tae protect ye're men, detective Raymond. If the mon's theory is richt and he has found some proof of it, they could be vera dour. I wadna take a chance."

Charlie Raymond nodded his head thoughtfully. "Are you saying the two might be in danger?"

"Aye."

"You could be right. Thank you. See you at 4:30?"

"Aye, indeed. I'm being relieved at 3:00 o'clock."

The men parted company.

In the room the two detectives met Edgar Vernon. They paused to take in the scene.

Edwin was swathed in white, still unconscious. He looked terrible to Charlie. He spoke to the man nevertheless, vowing to carry on with the case. He told him about the upcoming meeting with John Holmes Johnson. "Get well, my friend," he said softly.

Charlie turned as someone touched his arm.

Celine Sarii Emerson looked into his eyes with her soft green ones, full of moisture. He took her hand and kissed it. "How are you, Celine?"

"All right." Her voice trembled. "Lee wants to see you, Charlie."

"He spoke?"

"Just now. He said, 'I need Charlie'.

Innes whistled at the picture perfect estate of Judge Greene as his partner drove up the long drive.

Charlie parked near the greenhouse.

"It is 2:00 o'clock, callan."

Charlie grunted.

The two walked all around the circular building from a distance of about twenty feet. They moved slowly, gaining perspective of the layout of the property and the position of the greenhouse relative to all the other buildings. They walked in grass except when they crossed the western driveway.

Behind the greenhouse, ten feet from the backdoor, lumber was neatly stacked just off the flagstone patio. There were six sacks of concrete mix, bags of sand, and a small barrel of nails. One sack of sand had apparently been dropped and broken open. Sand had leaked out from the edge of the driveway to the pile of materials. The near-empty sack had been tossed on top the stack carelessly, half the bag hanging over the edge spilling a neat pile beneath it.

As they stepped inside the greenhouse, their shoes carried in some of the sand.

They completed their look around, made a few notes, and left the premises. They would compare their notes with those made by their colleagues later.

Charlie wondered about the sand.

Disasters happen
Dropping onto someone's life
Like the bombs on Pearl Harbor
Or a loved one's instant death
Creating havoc

Chapter eight

Out of the Blue
January 7 & 8, 1943

In a small apartment above a grocery store on Nebraska Street in Kansas City, Kansas, a man finished applying black dye to his hair. He wrinkled up his nose at the smell and cursed in Spanish. He toweled it dry and cleaned up the mess he had made.

As he came out of the bathroom, his brother opened the front door and entered carrying a large sack full of grub. They sat down to eat and make plans.

There was little resemblance between the Juarez brothers aside from language. Juan was tall, lithe, with dark brown eyes, and very tanned skin except for the areas not exposed to the sun. There, he was clearly pale.

The black dye covered his brunette hair.

Eduardo was shorter, of stockier build, with swarthy skin,

black eyes and his hair was naturally black. At 30, he was eight years younger than his half-brother.

They laughed evilly as they talked about their night with Sandra Rose Grun while they ate. And then they proceeded to lay out a verbal blueprint for their next meeting, if one proved necessary.

*****

Charlie Raymond approached the young secretary at the Holmes Detective Agency. His partner stopped just inside the door.

Out of habit, Charlie showed the woman his badge and introduced himself.

"Mr. Johnson is expecting you, Detective Raymond." Julia rose from her chair to show them in.

"Lot me, lass," said Malcolm. He approached the small group from his office.

The three men shook hands. Malcolm led the way to the office of John Holmes Johnson.

He positioned himself by the right side of the wheelchair.

No one spoke for a few seconds while the dark brown eyes of Charlie Raymond met the equally intense gray eyes of Holmes. They scrutinized each other silently, each reading something important about the other, forming instantly an impression of hidden strength.

"John Holmes, meet KCK police Detective Charlie Raymond. John Holmes Johnson, Detective."

With minimal assistance from the Scotsman at his elbow, Holmes extended his right hand.

Charlie shook it and was surprised by the light squeeze, expecting a firmer grip.

As their hands separated, John Holmes' weak right hand fell limply to the desk, knocking over a nearly empty cup.

A momentary flush of embarrassment reddened the face of John Holmes.

He moved his right arm with his left; Charlie wiped up the spill.

"I am sorry."

Charlie merely nodded. "Mr. Johnson, this is my partner, Detective Innes Wallace."

Innes stepped forward and took the offered left hand.

"Very Scottish name, Mr. Wallace. You two know each other?" His eyes moved from Innes to Malcolm and then back again.

"Aye, callan. We met at Bethany Hospital. They had cam to see Edwin and Lee."

"I see. Have a seat, gentlemen. How may I help you?"

For ten minutes the four engaged in friendly conversation, learning a little about each other. They had not brought up the cases as yet.

There was a quiet moment.

"May I offer tea or coffee?"

"Thank you, Mr. Johnson," Charlie tipped his head, "that would be great."

"My name is Holmes. Please feel free to address me as Holmes." He tapped the fingers of his right hand on the desk pad. "I apologize for my right hand. Like an errant child, it fails to obey me on occasion."

Malcolm returned with a tray of the offered drinks.

"What is your preference, Detective Raymond?"

"The name is Charlie, and I would like coffee."

Malcolm turned to Innes.

"Coffee. Is that a scone I see on that platter? My mouth is watering."

A laughing Malcolm offered a scone to his countryman. "Aye, callan.

Scones ar popular heir. We hae another detective frae Great

Britain, George St. Giles. And ye, callan?" he said, offering the platter to Charlie.

After several bites, Charlie conceded that they were very good. He took another bite. "What does callan mean?" He paused, hand halfway to his mouth.

"Not to worry, partner. It means young man, that's all." Innes reached for another scone. "It's a compliment, old man."

Charlie grunted his disapproval of the use of 'old man,' but said nothing. Finished with his scone, he wiped his mouth and hands. He picked crumbs from his rumpled suit, much more fastidiously than one would expect based on his outward appearance. He leaned back and crossed his arms.

Innes watched his partner. The man was quicker, smarter, and more discerning than his demeanor implied and so too, was this man in the wheelchair. Charlie likes Holmes, thought Innes.

Charlie Raymond glanced at his partner before speaking to Holmes.

"Lee Emerson spoke to us at the hospital today."

*****

All the way home that night, Holmes contemplated the information Detective Raymond had supplied concerning the attack on Edwin and Lee. He thought about Sandra Rose, which caused his thoughts to turn to Samantha. He wanted very much to hold her, to tell her how much he loved her.

He opened his eyes and looked out the car window but it was too dark. "Malcolm?" he said eagerly. "We are there?"

"Nae yit, callan. We've awa, air we get hame." He chuckled. "Anxious ar ye?"

"I am hungry."

"Hungry indeed. Donsy for a keek at ane canty lady, or the ither kind of hungry?"

A low rumble from the back seat filled the silence for half a second.

John Holmes laughed heartily before answering the Scotsman's query.

"Both. And you?"

"Aye, my lad. I am vera hungry too. The lo wad be welcome also. The nicht is cauld. Vera cauld."

"Yes."

"Here is the close noo. Hame at last."

Malcolm wheeled Holmes into the library where Samantha sat in a green La-Z-Boy wrapped in a red blanket. The fire filled the room with its cheerful glow and the snapping of the burning wood was like music.

"Look, Malcolm. Another Christmas present."

Samantha transferred to her husband's lap.

Malcolm left them to seek out his bonnie wife. He followed his nose to the kitchen.

Nuzzling the back of Marian's neck, Malcolm Macdougal whispered in her ear.

Turning into the big man's arms, she said, "Na, noo, lo'e. Supper first, then dessert." She gave him a big kiss and then returned to her job of cooking chicken for their evening meal.

"Lot me help?"

"Of course. You may mash the potatoes. Go wash, please."

"Aye, lass."

He left the room singing, "My love is like a red, red rose, that's newly sprung in June; oh my love's like the melody, that's sweetly played in tune. As fair art thou, my bonnie lass, so deep in love am I…"

He passed beyond her hearing but she knew the words by Robert Burns by heart. Marian wiped away tears and glanced around the kitchen which would, in due time, truly be hers. "When the new house is finished," she said out loud.

Malcolm walked in, freshly scrubbed and wearing a clean shirt.

"What did ye say, lo'e?"

"I was addressing the kitchen, soon to be our own, and in our house.

We can invite my family here. It will be so wonderful."

Marian cried for a brief time in the arms of her husband, and the hazel eyes of the tough detective glistened.

"Enough of this." She wiped her eyes and then dabbed Malcolm's with her apron.

The two busied themselves.

When all was ready and on the table, Malcolm went to the library to announce dinner. He made noise as he approached the door to let the couple know that he was coming.

Even so, when he knocked at the open door he saw Holmes removing his hand from under Samantha's sweater. His shirt was unbuttoned. The red blanket had been discarded and lay crumpled on the carpet.

A laughing Samantha buttoned her husband's shirt, straightened his hair with her hands and gave him one last kiss.

"Malcolm, help me up, will you?"

"Stay put, lass. I'll wheel ye baith."

"Great idea" said an enthusiastic Holmes. He tightened his grip. "Come on darling, it will be fun."

"Fun for you perhaps, sonsy mon. Together, we three weigh a ton, my darling."

Malcolm started to push the chair but it would not move.

Samantha laughed before she released the brakes. She began to cough and laid her head on John Holmes' shoulder, face turned away from him, her right arm encircling his neck.

"Tired, darling?"

"Yes." She said, but sighed wearily. "I must eat, however.

I am very tired of having no energy. Every little thing drains me."

"It's only been three days, darling. It takes a time for the medication to do its job. You will feel better, soon."

Marian giggled at the parade entering the dining room. She assisted Samantha to her seat at the table.

After Holmes blessed the food, Marian served.

Samantha ate only a few bites of the chicken but asked for seconds on the mashed potatoes. "What is this, Marian? It's different. I love it."

"Ye are eating colcanon, Samantha. A Scottish dish. Mashed potatoes with cabbage. I love it too, my bonnie lass." He grinned at his wife and winked.

"Cold-cannon?" asked Samantha.

"Na, lassie…kol'can'un, with a u."

"Kol'can'un, with a u." Samantha said it two more times just to make sure she was saying it properly.

A grinning Holmes said, "I think she's got it."

Everyone chuckled.

The evening ended pleasantly. At 9:00 o'clock, Marian helped Samantha prepare for bed and then tucked her in. She left the couple.

"I'm going to sit at my desk a wee, darling. I want to write a letter to Francois." He kissed his wife's forehead.

"All right. Oh my!"

"What's wrong?"

"The baby is kicking." She took his hand and moved it to her abdomen.

It was 9:45 before he actually made it to his desk. Half way through his letter to the Frenchman in New York, he stopped, lost in a line of thought totally unrelated to its completion.

He absentmindedly twirled the globe on his desk, staring at the land of his birth across the ocean, and for a minute he caressed the small bump representing Great Britain. He twirled the globe again, stopping it on North America. He tapped Mexico.

Getting out a fresh sheet of paper, he wrote an inquiry about the whereabouts of a Mrs. Robert Brian Bartlett, given name, Cynthia Bartlett and her five-year-old son, Robert Brian. Finished, he called Malcolm.

He was in bed by 11:00 o'clock but was unable to fall asleep until after 1:00. His thoughts were churning.

*****

In a Kansas City, Kansas hospital, George St. Giles sat outside the room of Sandra Rose Grun. The elder Gruns had been persuaded to go home to get some rest, escorted by William Leonard.

George finished his last bite of the two sandwiches William had provided.

He poured coffee from the thermos beside his chair and took three swallows before pulling the letter from his pocket. It was from his sweetheart in Springfield, Missouri. He looked up the empty hallway, sat his cup down, and then opened the letter from Georganne Hardy.

Georganne was a police officer in Springfield. They had met when he was in that town on the Shirley Poplin case. George sighed as he read. "Dearest George, I can barely wait for my birthday the fourteenth of February when you will be here to help me celebrate. You are the best thing that has ever happened…"

George dropped the letter at a loud cry of distress from inside the room. He rushed inside to gather a frightened, crying woman into his arms. He hit the call button.

Sandra Rose was screaming hysterically and fighting him, trying to extricate herself from his grip. Two nurses ran in; one left again to call the doctor on duty, while the second one helped

George. The nurse talked to the distraught woman, trying to get the message through that she was safe in a hospital.

After a sedative, she quieted and went back to sleep. She had not opened her eyes. George retrieved his possessions and sat by the bed all night.

At 6:00 o'clock Friday morning, Sandra Rose woke up. She glanced around and knew where she was. She watched the tiny stream of sunlight inching its way into the room through the window. She was so glad to see even this small bit of sunlight after her black ordeal and hours in a dark pit. Tears rolled down silently.

A small sound from her right caused her to turn that way. She was startled at the sight of a man. He was slumped in a chair, asleep. Her eyes slowly worked their way up the figure from the neatly manicured hands folded on his abdomen, to his chest with its dark gray tie, to his face. It was a nice face; young and clean shaved, with dark, straight brown hair falling down onto his forehead. This was not one of the men.

Relieved beyond measure, she could not hold back the surge of emotion any longer. She cried uncontrollably, in loud, gasping sobs.

George sat up but did not touch her. He gently handed her his handkerchief and waited.

Five minutes struggled by sliced up into chucks by her painful sobs.

Tears ceased to flow and dry sobs shook her body. Her chest hurt. "Who are you?" It was no more than the whisper of a soft summer breeze through pine trees.

"Detective George St. Giles, ma'am. I work with John Holmes and Samantha Johnson."

She continued to look at him but said nothing.

"Should I call the doctor, ma'am?"

She shook her head. "My baby...?"

"The baby is all right, ma'am."

"Please, stop calling me ma'am." She sobbed. "Will you hold me?"

George sat on the edge of the bed and pulled her to him.

She cried on his shoulder for a long time.

At 7:00, a nurse entered. For a while the room was busy with nurses and doctors. George resumed his seat outside the room.

When a breakfast tray arrived at 8:30, Sandra asked for George. He went in and she shared her breakfast with him.

Mr. and Mrs. Grun entered the room at 9:00.

After greeting the couple, George withdrew. He walked to the nurses' station and called the Agency.

Holmes and Malcolm were talking when Julia peeked in the office door. "George at Bethany, boss."

"Thank you, Julia." He picked up the phone and listened to the young detective's report. He hung up.

"Sandra Rose is awake."

Malcolm wheeled his boss out of the office.

It was 9:35 when Malcolm pushed his boss onto the hospital elevator. Before the door could close, a tall man in a brown suit stepped in; the elevator began to move.

The man stared at Holmes a second. "Detective Robert Wright, KCMOPD. We talked on the telephone. You are John Holmes Johnson?"

"Indeed so. Quite right. Good to meet you, Robert. My associate, Malcolm Macdougal. You are going up to talk to Sandra Rose?"

"Yes." He put his hand out. "Macdougal, nice to meet you. You are a Scotsman?"

"Aye, in a manner of speaking, callan?"

Robert Wright flashed a toothy grin. "That means young man. I happen to be good friends with Innes Wallace."

"Indeed! We have met."

They got off the elevator. At the room they met George and

all shook hands. George entered the room first to announce the arrival of the trio of detectives.

The elder Gruns went out to make room.

"I'll take them to the cafeteria for coffee, Holmes. Come, go with us, Malcolm?"

"Yes, Malcolm, go with them. I will fill you in. That is, if Robert will be good enough to push me."

"No problem."

The two entered and stood quietly and respectfully by the bed.

Pale and bruised but fresh in a clean gown, new bandages, and her hair combed, Sandra looked so much better then the last time Holmes had seen her.

He told her so as he took her hand.

Another minute of silence elapsed.

"I am sorry..." he stopped as she squeezed his hand.

"Be quiet Mr. Johnson. How could you have known this would happen? I had no inkling of such a thing." She shook her head. "Perhaps this attack was unrelated?"

"Perhaps." He did not think so but said nothing.

"You are?"

After introductions, there was a pause. The nurse entered, did her vitals thing, and departed.

Robert Wright cleared his throat.

"Yes, I know. What happened?" Sandra rubbed her forehead with a bandaged hand. "We have to do this, I know that."

Robert got out his notebook.

"Blast it!" exclaimed Holmes.

"What is it?"

"I forgot. I can't take notes yet. My right hand is reluctant and I write way too slow. I need Malcolm or George."

"I'll share my notes." The two men exchanged nods.

"Go ahead Mrs. Grun. Take your time."

It was early. Sandra Rose put an x through December 29 on her large calendar as she did each day as it passed. She was exhausted but unable to get to sleep.

She went to bed at midnight but finally got up at 1:30 to sit at the kitchen table with coffee. Padding into the living room in her slippers, she returned with a framed photograph of Eric. She put her head on the table and sobbed quietly.

She dozed off at 1:55.

A neighbor, just home from work at 2:00 a.m. saw a car park two houses from the Grun residence. Two figures got out. Unconcerned, he went to bed.

The two figures, dressed in dark clothing, walked around to the back door. The tallest one peeked inside through a slit in the curtains. He nudged his partner.

They could see Sandra Rose, asleep at the table, back to the door. The shorter of the two took a key ring from his pocket and unlocked the door with a house key taken from the body of Eric Grun.

They slipped noiselessly inside.

Sandra was awakened abruptly by an arm around her throat. She was yanked up and out of her chair. She fought the arm, knocking the framed picture to the floor. Glass crunched under the feet of the man holding her.

She could not breathe or scream.

A tight blackness went over her head, covering her eyes. She was gagged.

The arm loosened. She jabbed the assailant in the stomach with her elbow. He doubled over; she ran, almost making it into the bedroom.

Hands grabbed her and a prickly chin nuzzled her neck from behind.

She struggled. Something fell just before a blow to her chin caused her to crumple.

Her attackers carried her inert body through the front door to their car and drove away.

Sandra woke up in blackness. The gag was gone. She screamed as cold hands touched her body. She was kissed and struck repeatedly until her mouth was bloody.

"Now, you be quiet, little lady, and we may let you live." The man kissed her forehead. "Understand?"

She nodded. He lifted her tied hands over his head.

And so her nightmare began.

There was little let up in the assaults from one or the other. One talked while he tormented, the other one only grunted like a pig. His breath was foul.

She smelled coffee and there was a fire burning. She tried to concentrate on these sensations and shut out the mauling from the two pairs of rough hands.

"It's 7:30. Getting light."

The man on top of her grunted his reply and left her.

She felt so soiled. The cloth over her eyes was soaked with tears.

"Time for us to go, little lady," said the voice of the tall one. "It's been fun." He lifted her and threw her over his shoulder.

A door opened. A blast of cold air struck her nude body like a blow.

She was carried into the frigid darkness. Even as he walked, he continued to fondle her. She threw up as he laid her on the ground.

One held her tied hands, the other her legs and she was lowered into something. She smelled damp earth.

"No, oh no, please."

"Sorry, can't very well let you go."

She was shivering violently.

Something landed on her.

"Here is your gown and your slippers. No use dressing you, you won't be needing them in a little while."

The other man grunted and then he laughed.

She tried to sit up.

"Whoops, can't let you do that, now can we?"

The one with the sour breath jumped into the pit. He pulled her arms up above her head. She was smothering under his weight. When he was finished, she couldn't move her arms.

"Why?" she whispered.

Laughing evilly, the heavy-handed man struck her chin and she was out.

*****

When she woke up, her face was uncovered but she stared into the blackness of an earthen pit covered over with something.

Sandra Rose lay in her dark prison for 24 hours, drifting in and out of consciousness. Finally, she did not wake up.

Wednesday morning at 8:00, a rancher called police to report that intruders had been in his cabin at the western edge of his spread and there was blood everywhere.

Police followed two sets of footprints to a pit in the ground covered over by a pile of boards. Inside was a battered Sandra. That discovery was at 9:00 a.m. December 30.

*****

The story told, an exhausted Sandra Rose Grun closed her eyes.

Robert Wright pushed the wheelchair out of the hospital room. There was no sight of the others, so the two went to the cafeteria.

The Gruns left them to sit with their daughter-in-law. George got the two men coffee and pie.

Neither Robert Wright nor Holmes said anything.

They drank the coffee gratefully and ate the pie hungrily.

"It was bad?"

"Yes, George, it was indeed, bad."

At 11:00, the group parted company. Robert walked to their car with them and promised Holmes a copy of his report. Malcolm and George traded places, George leaving the hospital, Malcolm staying.

Holmes was moody. He stared out the window of his office for two hours. His mind was busy.

"Therapy time, boss."

There was no response. George took the initiative, delivering him to the clinic by 1:00.

Harvey Williams, the wheelchair-bound veteran of Pearl Harbor, now a physical therapist, recognized the black mood his friend was in. He did his job in silence. Finished, he put his hand on John Holmes' chest and shook him.

Holmes looked into Harvey's face.

"Want to talk about it?"

*****

George picked his boss up at 3:00. He drove to the office and parked.

"Please, take me home, George. I need to see my wife."

*****

Detectives Raymond and Wallace spent the day talking to the employees at Judge Greene's estate.

Raymond had found something interesting in a locked metal box in the Judge's office.

Like a spider's web
The intricate fabric grows
By one slender filament
Adhering to another-
A pattern emerges

Chapter nine

Cobwebs
January 8-11, 1943

Charlie Raymond sat in the center cottage on the Greene estate across the kitchen table from Thomas Hall Uland. Wanda Rae sat to his left. Willa Teresa Uland brought coffee and then she sat down to his right. His partner stood in the arched doorway between kitchen and dining room.

The older detective looked around before speaking. Mrs. Uland kept a neat house. The unit had no standard sized windows because it was sandwiched between the two end cottages. It was not dark however. The roof was a foot higher than the other cottages. Each room had two long, narrow windows in that space. The south end of the home had an extra large window to let in maximum sunshine.

"Can you get on with this, detective? We do have work to do."

"Of course, Mr. Uland." Charlie got out his black notebook and took a brown envelope out of his inside jacket pocket.

He started out with non-threatening questions; names, ages, length of service, any other children, and where they had been born, if not in Kansas City, Kansas.

The Uland's answered politely.

Charlie took a drink of his coffee.

Innes spoke. "When were you married, Mrs. Uland?"

"May 30 of 1920."

"Thomas worked here?"

"No. He was on leave from the service." For the first time, Willa Teresa looked nervous as though she could predict where this line of questioning would lead.

"How long were you home on leave, Thomas? Were you home again that same year?"

"Two weeks, and no." He looked exasperated. "Look, what does all this have to do with Judge Greene's death?"

"Your baby was born the second of April of 1921," said Charlie quietly.

The man sat very still, his face blank, unable or unwilling to address the implication of the fact. He looked at his wife.

"You went to San Francisco for two weeks in July, 1920 to spend time with Thomas, Willa?"

There was no answer.

Thomas shook his head. "I have never been to San Francisco."

Charlie opened the brown envelope and removed its contents. He laid them out neatly on the table.

"Notes from Willa Teresa to Judge Greene, train ticket stubs to and from San Francisco, California. They were purchased April 26, 1920. A hotel receipt for a Mr. and Mrs. Jordan for a ten-day stay. Two bank books with regular deposits of $1000 a year," Charlie made eye contact with Willa, "for twenty-one years."

The woman closed her eyes.

"One is in your name, Willa, and the other is your daughter's." He laid a photograph on the table. "A photo of you and the Judge snapped by a restaurant employee. Shall I go on?"

Willa shook her head. "No." She wiped her eyes with her napkin.

Thomas Uland's face changed. "I don't believe it," he said incredulously. "I can't believe this." His tone reflected his sudden surge of anger. "How could I have been so dumb."

"I was young and pretty. You were gone. I was hungry for love and attention." Willa sighed as her daughter began to sob. "The Judge was handsome, sweet, attentive…Mrs. Greene traveled frequently, taking their sons to New England where her family lived. In 1920, the boys were 15, 13,12, and 8. Kenneth was in college. They were gone all Summer." She sobbed as she said, "He took me with him to San Francisco." Her voice dropped to a whisper. "Leroy Greene is your father, Wanda."

"I know, mother."

There was a stunned silence.

"But, how?"

The silence grew fatter.

Thomas sulked. Willa cried; Wanda stared at her lap.

"The Judge objected to your engagement to Seadon Wells. Why?" asked Charlie.

Wanda fingered the ring on her left hand. "He called me into his study December 22. He told me I could not marry Seadon, that he would fire him if I didn't break it off. I told him that he had no right to tell me what to do and we would both quit before submitting to his demands."

"That's when he told you he was your father?"

"Yes. I was skeptical but he had proof." She waved a hand at the evidence spread out on the table.

"You told Seadon?" asked Innes.

Wanda raised her eyes to look at the detective. "Yes."

"How did Seadon react?"

Wanda looked at Charlie Raymond, clearly upset. "He was angry. Oh but, sir, he would never have killed the Judge. He wouldn't do that." She began weeping and shaking her head no.

"Where would Seadon be right now? I'd like him to join us here." Charlie addressed his question to Thomas.

"I'll call their cottage. He may be there. If not, he is in the garden somewhere."

Thomas went to the telephone. "On his way over. I told him to just walk in."

As he passed the young girl, she stood up.

"Daddy?"

"It's all right, baby." He hugged his daughter of twenty-one years. "It's all right. You are my little girl, regardless."

They were still hugging when Seadon entered the kitchen. Wanda went to him.

His face clouded. "You know?" he asked Charlie.

"Yes."

"What did you do when you were threatened by the Judge?"

"What do you mean, what did I do? I told him to back off or I would tell Kenneth."

"Did you kill him?" Charlie said it very nonchalantly.

Seadon's face blanched.

"Damn it any way, detective. Stop this right now. I killed Judge Greene. I killed him. He had no cause to fire Seadon nor prevent them from marrying. Wanda was so miserable. I confronted him in his haven, the greenhouse" Thomas Hall Uland added, "I'll make a statement and sign it."

"No daddy. Don't do this."

"You like to tell us how you did it, Mr. Uland?"

"No. You figure it out." He looked smug and very satisfied with his suggestion.

"You have something you want to say, Seadon?"

"He didn't do it, sir. I did it."

Wanda looked at the two most important men in her life, and then ran out of the room crying with unrestrained anguish.

Willa stood up.

"Go with her, Mrs. Uland.

*****

Saturday, Malcolm drove Holmes to the Hobert residence to speak to Nevin. The three brothers followed their father into the living room.

"What is this about?" asked Cal.

"We talked to Janette Tomlinson, Nevin. She says you two were not together Saturday the 26th because you broke up with her on the 19th. You lied to us."

"I didn't lie. Just a mistake, that's all. Got the dates mixed up, so what. Why would I lie?"

"Indeed. Why would you lie?"

"Could it be that ye were a wee jealous, lad? Ye didna like ye're brether's friendship with Eric Grun nor his affair with Lucille Sloan."

The Hobert men focused their eyes on the youngest of their clan, questioning him without sound.

The brash young blond reacted angrily. "Why do you look at me like that? None of you approved of Lucille any more than I did. Doesn't mean I killed her, for Christ's sake."

"Don't use the Lord's name…"

"Stop telling me how to talk and how to think, Pop. Stop bossing me around. You all do it, all of you."

He jumped to his feet and backed away from his siblings.

"Faxon never orders me around. He treats me like I got brains and feelings." He paused for breath.

"Want to tell us what this is?" said Holmes. He held out a small packet the size of a Hersey bar.

Nevin reacted as though struck. He swatted the packet out of John Holmes' right hand. The falling package opened to shower several accordion-folded sheets of printed material across the floor.

Cal Hobert retrieved three of them. He handed one to his brother, Lloyd, and another to his father.

Holmes gasped as his strengthless arm struck the wheelchair handle. Pain crossed his face. He hugged the arm to him.

"Callan, ar ye stound?" Malcolm glared at Nevin. "Ye ar ae lucky lad, I dinna want to start a collie shangie. I wad lik tae pack ye sweerly for this. Ye ar ane ramstam. Ye hae punced his thewless nieve." Malcolm stepped forward menacingly.

The boy shrank back, up against the wall.

"No, Malcolm. Leave him be."

"Aye."

"Can I get you something, Holmes?" asked J.B.

"Aspirin?"

"Done."

"What did Malcolm say?" asked Lloyd Hobert.

Holmes looked at Lloyd and translated his friend's words. "He said, 'You are one lucky fellow, I don't want to start a brawl. I wud lik tae hit you heartily for this. You are one headstrong fellow. You have hurt his weak arm.' Close enough, my friend?"

"Aye, callan. I'm sary I lost me birse…my temper."

Rubbing his right arm and chuckling at his friend's stream of words, Holmes addressed the Hoberts. "When Malcolm gets upset, he reverts to his Scottish dialect. Makes him a wee hard to understand sometimes."

J.B. Hobert handed him two aspirin and a glass of water

and then watched him take them. Lloyd placed an ice pack on the arm.

Holmes blushed at the fuss being made over him.

J.B. glared at his youngest.

"I'm sorry," he said belligerently. "I'm sorry, Mr. Johnson," he repeated softer.

Nevin picked up one of the sheets of paper. Keeping his eyes on it as he talked, he tried to explain them. "You are right. I was jealous of Eric Grun. the man was so friendly, so sure and confidant. He was usurping my place as Faxon's best friend. I decided to make him look bad. I printed these up and distributed them. I just laid them all around to be found by the crews the next day." He ripped the paper in half. "I didn't expect him to be fired."

The young man's eyes stared at the Englishman. "I did not kill him, sir."

Holmes nodded once. "Who reported him for 'un-American activities' other than the pamphlets?"

J.B. answered. "One of our foremen, Juan Juarez. He and his brother, Eduardo, were apparently targeted by Eric for hate messages and their car was vandalized."

"May we speak to them?"

"Of course." J.B. shuffled some papers. "They will be at a construction site in Olathe, Monday. I'll give you directions."

"Don't be surprised, Nevin, if Detective Joel Anderson shows up to ask you the same questions we just did. He won't just sit back and assume Faxon guilty. He will look for proof." Holmes looked at the bruise forming on his right wrist. "Have you ever been to Lucille Sloan's house?"

"No way. Of course not."

Five men looked daggers at him. His stubborn attitude melted.

"Yes."

Holmes nodded. "If they find your fingerprints..." he left the sentence dangling.

Malcolm drove back to the estate.

Samantha greeted her husband with tenderness and love. She massaged the bruised arm. They soaked it while sitting in front of the fireplace, dreaming about their new home to be.

Monday morning, George and Malcolm drove to Olathe and sought out the construction site. Typical of a site of heavy building activity, it was crowded with equipment, piles of materials, and tools. The two men walked around the area for a half-hour before searching out the Juarez brothers.

Malcolm nudged George. He pointed. Off to one side was a large yellow flat bed truck filled with the rough lumber used to frame up the foundations and pillars before concrete was poured.

They walked around it.

"Broken headlight," said George.

"Aye, and black paint smears."

"Let's find the foremen, shall we?"

"Indeed, callan."

They walked on. A workman directed them to a shabby trailer.

George knocked.

The door opened.

"Juan Juarez?"

"No, señor. Esta aqui." He waved inside. They entered as he was putting on his hard hat. He left.

A tall man with a dark complexion, black hair and dark eyes, looked up from a desk littered with papers.

They talked for twenty minutes. He confirmed the story about Eric Grun.

"We wad lik to see ye're car."

"We are also interested in a truck on the south side of the site. It may have been involved in a hit and run."

"Let me see it, señors. Then I can find out where it has been and who has driven it."

"Thank you for your cooperation, Señor Juarez. You were born in Mexico?" George had asked it out of genuine curiosity but as he watched the guarded look cross the man's face, he wondered why.

Malcolm had noticed too.

They exchanged looks as they followed the man out of the trailer.

*****

As they approached the truck, Juan called out loudly, "Eduardo?"

"Aqui."

"Un momento, por favor," he said to the two detectives. He walked a few feet away. The two brothers spoke in rapid Spanish.

A smiling Juan rejoined them. "Mi hermano…lo siento mucho. My brother, Eduardo. To answer your question, señor, we were born in Mexico. We moved to Los Estados Unitos after the…muertos…the deaths of our parents." He looked around. "Where is this truck, señor?"

They looked the truck over carefully. Juan looked inside at a clipboard.

"Si, this truck was in Kansas city that week. The engine needed some work. Come, we will look up the driver." He started back toward the office.

Malcolm glanced at his watch. It was 9:40. Something struck the back of his head. He fell forward into George.

The big man shook his head like a bull in the ring. Two more blows drove him to his knees. He watched a 2"x2" strike George. On his knees, he could only see legs and muddy, heavy duty boots. A fist pounded him in the face. He saw the board coming at his head but he was powerless to ward it off as his arms were held as by a vise. The board struck the right side of his head and he swam in black pain. He hit the ground hard. A steel pointed boot grazed his temple and struck him hard above the right ear. I am dead, he thought.

George was likewise being bombarded with blows from several men. Juan Juarez grabbed his hair and sneered at the bloodied Englishman. "So, you and your nosy countryman are doomed. Sweet dreams, señor." Juan hit him with such viciousness that the victim's head flew back into the chin of one of the men holding him. The man crumpled with a bloody mouth.

George fell beside his friend.

An angry Eduardo, with mouth and chin covered with blood, kicked him three times in quick succession.

Yelling orders in Spanish, Juan directed the clean-up operation. He had to erase all traces of the assault. He sent his brother to clean himself up while the other eight men tidied up the area. The brutally beaten men were put in their car and Juan himself, towed it away. Behind him he could see his crew hosing down the bloody ground and burning the bloody weapons.

Juan drove north on Highway 7 to Highway 40, west a half-mile and then north again on a gravel road. In the middle of nowhere, no house visible in any direction, he stopped. He unchained the car from his truck, set the brake, and then pulled his vehicle forward. He walked back to the car, pulling on a pair of gloves. Reaching inside past the body of George St. Giles, slumped in the driver's seat, he started the car. He released the parking brake and pushed the car off the road. It rolled downhill into a stand of ancient trees. "Adios, muchachos."

Satisfied, he got in his truck and drove back to the site by a round-about path, singing several popular Mexican tunes as he drove.

"Going to be a cold day," he said happily to his reflection in the mirror. He wiped a small spot of blood from his cheek.

*****

John Holmes Johnson looked at the clock in his office for the fifth time-it was 12:25 and still no Malcolm and George. "Where are you?" he said aloud as he rubbed his bruised wrist. "No Samantha, no Malcolm, no George, and no William. How do I get to the clinic?" He tapped the desk.

Holmes picked up the phone with his left hand, laid it on the desk, and dialed.

After three short phone calls, he looked at his watch again. It was 1:05. His office door opened.

"Malcolm?"

"No, boss." Julia and Jewell entered. "No sign of them and no calls."

"Come on. We are taking you to Myra's clinic. I called her to let her know that you would be a little late."

"But..."

He was wheeled out before he could formulate a protest.

At 4:45, Holmes still sat at his desk, wondering. The girls had left at 4:30.

At 5:15 he heard a key in the front door and then footsteps.

Isaac and Zeke Martin walked in, followed by the two secretaries.

"Come to take you home, boss." Isaac raised a hand to stave off any comment. "No use arguing. You, sir, are outnumbered."

"Quite right."

"Here we go."

"Any word?" asked Holmes as he was pushed into the elevator.

"Not yet," said Isaac.

"Police on both sides of the state line are searching, Holmes," added Zeke. He kept his hand reassuringly on John Holmes' shoulder.

No one that knew the two missing men, slept that night.

Carrie spent some time at the residence to help comfort Marian.

Holmes stayed home Tuesday, just waiting.

Isaac relieved William's guard duty at the hospital so that he could go home to be with his wife and George's grandmother, Veda.

It was to be a long night and a nerve racking morning.

An exhausted Marian finally dozed off at 3:00 a.m. on the brown sofa in the library.

When the doorbell rang at noon, Holmes was sleeping in his wheelchair while Samantha did the same in the La-Z-Boy. Kendall Wiles was sitting with the family. He hurried to the door before the bell could ring again.

Detectives Raymond and Wallace entered. They had heard about the disappearance and joined in the search.

Kendall led them to the library that doubled for a sitting room in the small house.

The two men found seats and just sat, reluctant to wake the family.

Kendall served coffee.

It was the aroma of the coffee and the tinkle of a spoon on a china cup that penetrated John Holmes' sleep. He jerked awake.

"Who's here?" The question was muffled.

"Kendall, sir. Have some coffee, Holmes?"

He helped Holmes get a firm grip with both hands before he told him about the visitors.

"Push me closer, Kendall."

Holmes spilled some coffee on his lap and looked in vain for a place to sit the cup.

Innes took the cup from him; Charlie handed him a napkin.

"They have been found?"

"Yes, Holmes." Charlie Raymond sat down again. "A rural postman found them off a gravel road off Highway 7, north of 40. Their car went off the road into some large trees at the bottom of a ravine."

Charlie paused at a cry from the sofa. Marian struggled to sit up. Awakened by the anguished cry, Samantha went to sit beside her.

"They are alive."

There was a finality to the words that surprised the two detectives from the Kansas side of the Missouri River.

"Yes, Holmes. How did you know?"

Holmes shrugged. "I didn't. I just know that we are a stubborn people, and Malcolm especially, would not die easily."

"Aye, Holmes. You are quite right. They had been severely beaten and then placed back in their car. The car was pushed off the road." Innes stood up. "Come, we will take you to them. They are in St. Margaret's hospital in Kansas City, Kansas."

After they drove away, Kendall walked to the main house to tell Carrie; my wife called me at the plant.

At 12:15, Joel Jacob Anderson was at William Leonard's house telling Veda Grantham about her grandson. He drove her to St. Margaret's.

According to the Juarez brother's and ten workers at the Olathe construction site, the detectives had never made it there. At the time, there seemed no reason not to believe them.

Anger blinds a man-
His is like tunnel vision
Seeking revenge at all cost
Sacrificing everything
To satisfy it

Chapter ten

Two Blind Mice
January 13-15, 1943

By the thirteenth, Lee Emerson was up and walking with crutches. Edwin Wylie Vernon had not yet come out of his coma. The younger detective had been transferred to the same room, and for that Lee was grateful. He cared deeply about his partner and mentor. The two families had grown very close over the ten years of their partnership.

Edgar Vernon visited his brother daily, without fail.

Lee wondered how Charlie and Innes were doing on the case. He sat down by his friend's bed to watch him breath, patiently waiting for the day the eyes would open.

Sandra Rose was released from the hospital at 1:00 o'clock.

She was taken out a back door, escorted by Isaac Martin and William Leonard. She did not go home.

Georganne Hardy, accompanied by her parents, Police

Chief Warren G. and Nara Lou Hardy, arrived from Springfield, Missouri at the same hour. They walked in the front door even as Sandra was taken out the back of Bethany Hospital.

*****

Juan Juarez hung up the telephone. As requested, the hospital staff had reported Sandra's condition as critical. Juan laughed as he dialed St. Margaret's. The report on the condition of the two British citizens was equally grim.

Juan left the trailer that was his office and searched out his brother.

"It is time to take out J.B. Hobert and vamoose."

*****

At police headquarters, only two blocks from the scene of the hit and run that had put their colleagues in the hospital, Charlie Raymond entered a small, windowless room. He sat down at a table opposite Seadon Wells.

Innes followed a minute later with three coffees.

"All right. Let's go back to December 22. When did Wanda tell you about her conversation with Judge Greene?"

"About 9:00 o'clock. I had picked her up at 7:00 and we were at dinner."

"Where?"

"We were at the Golden Ox. My cousin works there, I eat there frequently. I am well known."

"Go on."

"When she told me, I was angry and ready to confront him." He looked at his hands. "We went to a motel instead."

"I didn't hear that, Seadon," said Charlie gently.

"We went to a motel."

"You spent the night at a motel?"

Seadon shook his head no. "No, officer. We drove home,

arriving about 2:30 a.m. Our families live in very close proximity. We couldn't spend the night together-we couldn't do that to them."

"Let's move on. You talked to the Judge...when exactly?"

"It was Friday, sir. The Judge was gone all day Thursday and he and Mrs. Greene were gone all evening at a Christmas party. Kenneth and his wife were gone also. Wanda baby-sat with the children. On Friday I went to the Judge's study at 9:00 a.m. with coffee and apple pie-from my mom. It was a regular practice of the Judge to take refreshment at that time. I confronted him. We had words." The Judge suggested that we postpone our quarrel. "'Let's hash this out after Christmas,'" he said, "'so we won't spoil everyone's holiday'". He suggested that the three of us meet on the 26th." Seadon rubbed the back of his neck.

"You agreed?"

"Yes, as strange as it may seem to you, detective. I had no more desire than he did to throw all this at the families on Christmas Eve. I agreed to keep it to myself until after we had our meeting."

"You had no problem with this?" asked Innes.

"No, sir. The Judge can be very persuasive. Besides that, he was right. This altercation would ruin everyone's holiday-my parent's, Wanda's family, and it was reasonable to assume that neither Mrs. Greene nor Kenneth Greene knew about the liaison between Willa Teresa and the Judge. We were to meet at 3:00 o'clock Saturday the 26th in the study."

"Why so late in the afternoon?" asked Charlie.

"My family was gone all day Friday visiting relatives. The same was true of the Ulands. Everyone slept late Saturday morning. It was a regular part of our holiday. No one was required to resume his or her duties until 9:00 o'clock. There was also a scheduled delivery of building materials that morning, at the greenhouse." He shrugged. "Maybe it was just to give us time to calm down and be able to discuss it rationally. I don't know. It did not bother me, nor did it bother Wanda. She was not anxious to have the fact made public that she was the illegitimate child of Judge Leroy Greene."

Innes spoke up just then. "Back up a little. Tell us about the delivery of building materials."

Seadon leaned back in his chair and looked thoughtful. "Why?"

"Just humor us, Seadon."

"If you insist. The Judge intended to build onto his green house and add an arbor. I saw the truck arrive at 8:55 as I was walking from my cottage to the main house. I saw two men get out of the truck. The taller of the two went to the back door of the greenhouse. The other one stood by the back of the flat-bed truck, waiting."

"What color truck? Can you describe it to us?" asked Innes.

"Why?"

"How about more coffee, Innes. Would you like some, Seadon?"

"Yes, please."

Innes returned in less than five minutes.

Charlie took a sip of the strong, slightly bitter drink. He shook his head sadly. "What I would give for a cup of your wife's wonderful, freshly brewed coffee, Innes."

"Aye."

"Where did you go to college, Seadon?"

Seadon looked surprised for a second, but than he laughed. "Kansas State Teacher's College in Emporia, sir. I have a degree in Education with emphasis on English literature. How did you know, sir?"

"Who else would say 'altercation' instead of argument and 'liaison' instead of affair?" Charlie Raymond nodded knowingly.

The three men shared a rare moment of camaraderie.

Setting his cup down carefully, Charlie Raymond wiped his hands on his handkerchief and returned to business. "We are trying to help you, Seadon. Help us even if you don't understand the question."

The young man drank half the bitter drink before speaking. "Right. It had a yellow cab, black flatbed. It came in the west driveway and parked next to the greenhouse. I saw the Judge come outside and talk to the men, presumably to tell them where to pile the materials. He went back inside. The men started unloading."

"Any words on the truck?"

"May have been words. If so, I did not notice."

"Descriptions?"

"One was shorter than the other. The tallest one was the same height as the Judge. They were bundled up in brown jump suits, collars up, gloves and heavy boots. I couldn't see the men. The truck left at 10:20."

"Both men were in the truck?"

Seadon just looked at Charlie, perplexed by the question.

"Did you actually see two men leave?"

"No, sir. I just saw the back of the empty truck. I was in the parlor helping my father."

"One more question, Seadon. "When you found the Judge, did you go in the south or north door?"

"The south door, sir. The one closest to the deck."

Charlie nodded his head and said, "Ah."

The two detectives left their office at 3:45, headed for the Holmes Detective Agency.

At the office, Samantha Jewell dabbed her eyes as she addressed Charlie Raymond. "I am sorry, detective. The boss went to Olathe to see the construction crew there."

"How?"

"My husband, Isaac Martin, drove him." She sighed. "I'm a little worried."

"Nothing to worry about, my dear. If you will give us directions, we will head that way too."

Back in their car, Charlie said tensely, "Step on it, Innes. I have a bad feeling about this."

"Aye, callan."

Charlie grunted.

As Innes sped across town toward the site of a new motel on the southern edge of Olathe, Kansas, Isaac was pulling up close to the battered green trailer. He parked.

"Hope I didn't run over any nails, boss. I hate changing flat tires."

"Understandable. I hate changing tires too." John Holmes suddenly laughed.

Isaac grinned at his boss through the open back door. "What's so funny."

Holmes waved a hand. "It just occurred to me that I have never, ever changed a tire in my life."

The younger man laughed. "Trust me, boss. You would hate it. I'll see if someone is here. Sit tight."

"Sit tight? Does that mean don't move?"

Isaac chuckled as he approached the trailer door. It opened even as he knocked.

"Juan Juarez?"

"Si, señor, and you are?"

"Isaac Martin from the Holmes Detective Agency. My boss, John Holmes Johnson would like a word with you, if possible."

"Of course. Come in."

"Perhaps you will come to the car, señor? Mr. Johnson is confined to a wheelchair and…" he gestured at the narrow stairs.

"Si, I am happy to oblige." The man followed Isaac to the

car. He saw his brother headed toward them so he waved him off, not wishing to explain about Eduardo's cut lip and chin.

Isaac opened the door and Juan climbed in to sit by Holmes.

"What do you want, Señor Johnson?"

Holmes looked into the dark brown eyes for a second and shuddered.

"Let me shut the door, boss. Any objection, senor?" Isaac waited for a reply.

"No objection. If you choose to abduct me, there are ten husky men here who would strongly oppose it." Juan laughed without humor. "I am a busy man, Señor Johnson."

"Quite right. My apologies. Two of my agents were found..."

"Si. The dos hombres found injured north of here. I have already talked to the police, señor. Your men were not here." He shrugged. "What more can I tell you?" He reached for the door handle.

"Un momento, señor. Perhaps you will answer the questions they would have asked..." he paused briefly, "had they made it here. We are investigating the death of Eric Grun, and the abduction of his wife, Sandra Rose. Por favor, señor."

"Very well. Get on with it then."

After a ten minute discussion of the alleged verbal and violent, racially motivated abuses he and his brother had been subjected to, the conversation ended abruptly.

"I must get back to work." Juan Juarez opened the door, anxious to rid himself of this nuisance of a man.

As he climbed out, Holmes addressed him again.

"What about your car, Robert?"

Once out of the car, Juan turned to look inside, and answered smoothly.

"Me llamo Juan. Mi hermano es Eduardo. What about my car, señor?" The dark eyes did not flinch.

"My apologizes. I understood it had been vandalized. Perhaps I was wrong."

"It was vandalized. He slashed the seat cushions and did minor damage to the engine. It has been repaired. You must excuse me now, gentlemen. Adios."

He slammed the door hard and stomped off toward the place he had last seen his brother.

The two detectives watched him until he disappeared before they drove away.

John Holmes leaned back in his seat, suddenly tired.

"I don't like that man, boss."

"Nor do I, Isaac. Take me home, please."

"Yes, sir." He looked in the mirror at the grimace on the man's face. "I'm sorry, Holmes. A slip of the tongue."

Isaac helped Holmes into his residence and drove away to go home to his wife.

Sue Foster, wife of Washington, was at the house with Samantha in the absence of Marian. She hugged the man affectionately before pushing his chair into the library. She left him sitting by the reclining chair watching his wife sleep.

Back in the kitchen, Sue continued to prepare supper. Her husband entered from the storage area that had once been the apartment of Marian Baker before she had become Mrs. Macdougal.

Washington hugged his wife and handed her a hothouse-bred tulip.

At 5:30 everything was ready and on the table.

The thirty four-year-old man with the mahogany skin of his Native American ancestors and the black hair and eyes of his Sioux mother, went to the library on silent feet.

*****

Holmes sat in front of the fire rubbing his forehead, his eyes tightly shut. Nevertheless, he said, "Come in, Washington."

Washington chuckled quietly. "How did you know it was me, sir?"

"Footsteps, Washington."

"Footsteps, sir?"

"Yes, Washington. You have a distinctive footfall, very soft and hard to hear, and there is an unusual pattern to it. You slightly drag your left foot. A childhood injury no doubt."

Washington laughed. "Right you are. Dinner is ready, sir."

"Please, Washington…"

"I know, Holmes. Drop the 'sir' stuff." He took over the wheelchair as Holmes labored to move it closer to Samantha.

Holmes touched his wife gently. "Dinner, darling."

The four ate together.

At 7:00 o'clock, Holmes called the hospital.

*****

By the time Charlie and Innes arrived at the construction site, Holmes had come and gone as had the Juarez brothers.

While they talked to a young man about twenty, Charlie Raymond looked around him.

"What is your name, son?"

"Me llamo Hector Sanchez, señor."

"Hector?"

The friendly young man grinned and turned his yellow hard hat round and round in his callused hands. "Si, señor." He shrugged. "What can I do?"

"Tell me, Hector, any visitors been here this evening?"

"Dos hombres, señor. They talk, they leave. Then the boss leave."

"His brother leave with him?" asked Innes.

Hector nodded affirmatively.

"Any objection if we look around, Hector?"

"No, señor. I have no objections. The light is not good. You had better hurry."

"That's true. Get the flashlights, Innes."

Hector stood, nervously chewing his lower lip. The hat rotated faster.

"What is it, Hector?" Charlie did not look at the young man.

"You would perhaps like to start over there by that pile of rough boards, señor." He barely moved his head to their left and rolled his eyes the same way.

Charlie said a whispered, "Thank you."

Hector hurried away.

The two men walked slowly to their left. There was a large rectangular area, clean of snow as though something had been parked there.

"There was a truck here, Innes. My guess would be the hit and run truck."

"Wonder where it is now?"

The two men circled around with flashlights on. Once Charlie tripped and fell to one knee.

Innes helped him up.

"Blood on the snow," whispered Charlie.

"A spot they missed apparently."

They moved on.

Behind them, four pairs of black eyes watched.

Charlie Raymond was fully aware of the audience and he deliberately hammed it up for their benefit. Throwing up his arms in a gesture of frustration, he exclaimed, "There's nothing here. We're wasting time."

"Right." Innes followed his partner's lead, playing his flashlight over the snow as he walked. The whole area was a mass of tracks, of men and machine. The light struck something shiny. Innes slipped and dropped his flashlight in the snow edging the bare rectangle. "I don't believe it." He added a curse for good measure.

"Are you all right?" Charlie stopped and turned towards his partner, his light turned down toward the ground.

"Slipped and almost fell. Dropped my flash." Innes made a great show of picking up the light and brushing away the snow.

"Let's go home. I'm hungry." Charlie walked briskly to the car.

He kicked snow off his boots and climbed in the passenger side.

Innes got in and started the engine.

They drove away.

"What did you find?"

"A button." Innes handed it over.

Charlie examined it with his flash. "A coat button judging from its size. It has a thistle on it." He turned off the light. "That is the symbol of Scotland."

"Aye. Are you thinking what I am thinking?"

Innes drove straight to his house on 45th Street.

"Aren't you forgetting something, Innes? I live at 18th and Washington Street."

"You're coming to my house for dinner, old man. Wife's orders."

Charlie Raymond grunted at the term, 'old man.'

*****

Tuesday morning, Kendall Wiles drove Holmes to St. Margaret's Hospital to see Malcolm and George. They arrived at 9:15.

As Kendall pushed the wheelchair out of the elevator and down the corridor, they saw Doctor Joseph Billings entering a room down the hall. He waved their way. Holmes returned the gesture.

Kendall turned his back to the door and pushed, slowly pulling the chair through the opening. The weight of the door was suddenly removed from his back by someone in the room. He backed up to the space between the two beds so he could turn the chair.

Marian Macdougal rose from her chair and greeted the new arrivals warmly.

Kendall gave her a brief hug and pat on the back and then he moved aside to stand by the bed of the Scotsman.

Marian dropped to one knee to receive a big hug from John Holmes. He kissed both of her cheeks.

"Any change?"

She shook her head.

He kissed her hand.

Marian tried to push the chair up closer to the bed but there was not enough room.

"Here, Marian, let me help you."

Warren G. Hardy moved the empty chair and rolled the bedside tray out of the path of the wheelchair. He turned the wheelchair around and moved it backward until Holmes sat at the bedside of his friend.

John Holmes stared at the bruised face of his countryman without comment. His breathing quickened, his eyes misted, but he kept control. He managed to get his right hand up to the bed but could not maneuver it through the railing.

"Blast it!" All the frustrations of the last few days seemed to be packed into the soft but vehement words.

The room was quiet.

Marian took the right hand of her boss and hugged it to her left cheek where the scar of a bullet wound was. John Holmes shed tears, overwhelmed for a moment by the power of his sense of helplessness.

"Marian, I am so sorry."

"Hush, Holmes."

Warren G. put the offensive metal bar down and then placed the right hand of John Holmes on top of the injured man's left one.

"Thank you, Warren G. You brought Georganne?"

"That's right, Holmes. This is my wife, Nara Lou. Meet John Holmes Johnson, honey."

She took the offered left hand. "Good to meet you, John. I have heard a lot about you via my daughter."

She backed away; Georganne moved up, hugging him firmly. "George will be all right, don't you worry." She wiped his face discreetly as she added, "I do believe that he is as stubborn as you are, Holmes."

*****

Kendall delivered Holmes to his office at 10:30 and then drove back to the estate.

Alone in his office, John Holmes sat in silent contemplation for fifteen or so minutes before he picked up the telephone.

It rang four times before it was answered.

"Joel Anderson."

"Good morning, Joel. I received a letter from Mexico you will be interested in. Are you swamped today?"

"Yes, Holmes. We found Nevin's fingerprints on the basement door handle at Lucille's house. We are picking him up. Also, we discovered that Faxon lied about breaking it off with Lucille. Wanted his cake and his cookie at the same time, I guess." Joel chuckled.

"Joel, that's crass."

"Sorry, Holmes. We have an appointment with Faxon's fiancée at 2:00." He sighed, sounding tired. "How about tomorrow morning?"

"Fine. Breakfast at Judy's?"

"Sounds good. Joel, shall we invite Detectives Raymond and Wallace?"

"Right. I'll call them. Later, my friend."

Holmes sat a minute, tapping his fingers on the desk. Then he called Robert Wright.

John Holmes wrote in his laborious way with a right hand that tired quickly and sometimes jerked as he moved across the page. Going back to dot the i's and cross the t's was difficult so he had started leaving them off. The girls were getting very efficient at reading his odd writing.

Samantha Jewell had brought lunch so they avoided going out.

The office was gloomy.

At 3:00 o'clock, Charlie Raymond called.

"Hello, Charlie. I understand from my secretary that you followed me to the construction site yesterday. Sorry we missed each other."

There was silence on the phone.

"Charlie?"

"Here, Holmes. We missed the Juarez brothers too. A young man named Hector Sanchez gave us permission to look around."

"Indeed."

The man explained what they had found.

"George does have a wool coat made in Scotland," said a subdued Holmes.

"I checked his coat. The button came from it all right. No mistake."

"You have the Juarez brothers?"

"No, we haven't found them yet. No one at the site has seen them since yesterday. So they say. They left yesterday right after you did."

"We need to protect J.B. Hobert. I have a feeling…"

"He could be next. Good point."

"Talk to Joel Anderson?"

"Yes, I did. See you tomorrow."

*****

Isaac delivered Holmes to his residence at 5:00.

Samantha was recovering slowly.

She greeted him, rather passionately he was thinking. Her greeting chased away some of the gloom he was feeling.

After dinner, Sue Foster went back to her cottage to spend time with her husband.

Holmes called Owen Farmer at the stable and arranged a surprise for his wife.

At 7:00 o'clock Owen showed up at the door with a sleigh pulled by a chocolate brown mare. He helped the couple bundle up appropriately and then settled them into the vehicle. He spread wool blankets over the two, grinning as they kissed. A light snow was falling.

Owen drove slowly west on the recently added road and across the newly built bridge to the site of their new home to be.

He drove southward in the moonlight, urging the mare on as the wind blew the snow like fairy dust, for approximately twenty minutes.

The wind grew colder; he circled back.

"Stop, Owen. Let's just sit here a minute or two."

"Okay, boss. If you don't mind, I need to visit the outhouse."

"What outhouse?" asked Samantha.

"Hush, darling," said her husband as he kissed her again.

Owen chuckled as she pulled the blanket up over their heads.

He walked south of the deep pit that would be the foundation for their house. He stood with his back to the sleigh eating a chocolate bar but wishing it was a cup of hot chocolate. He shivered. Time to head back, he was thinking, just as a prickle at the back of his neck caused a feeling of apprehension to wash over him. He shivered again.

Something slammed into his back, and he was shoved forward violently into a tree. He dropped to his knees. His head slammed into the tree again.

Unconscious and gagged, Owen Farmer was tied to the tree, on his knees with arms around it and face against the rough bark.

Two figures moved stealthily toward the sleigh and the couple enjoying a romantic interlude.

The horse whinnied.

John Holmes heard a twig snap.

"Good timing, Owen. Let's go home."

There was no reply.

Samantha pulled the blanket away from their faces and straightened up in the seat. It was 8:40.

The two figures walked into their visual range like ghosts in the now heavily falling snow.

In seconds they were at the vehicle.

Eduardo pulled Samantha from the seat, holding her against him with one arm around her neck, the other over her mouth.

Juan Juarez grabbed John Holmes' left arm. "You will do as I say, señor, or the little lady is muerto. Entiende?"

"I understand."

Juan yanked Holmes hard and laughed as he landed face down in the snow.

Eduardo had Samantha tied and gagged. He pushed her toward the pit.

"No." Holmes tried to get up but the snow encrusted boot of the taller Juarez brother came down on his back and pressed him into the cold powder.

"You are next, señor. After the little lady."

In the center of the pit, the stocky man pushed Samantha down in a sitting position against a pile of snow covered earth. He tied her feet. A gloating, sneering man pulled the gag off long enough to kiss her roughly. His breath made her retch. He replaced the cloth and retraced his steps up the plank walk.

Eduardo dragged Holmes feet first, down the plank. Juan followed. The two carried him toward Samantha, dropping him face down, six feet away from her.

Seconds later they were gone, as was the plank.

All was gray. The snow was falling in huge flakes, the moonlight obscured, no sound, no wind. An eerie stillness prevailed.

There was no sound or movement from Holmes.

Samantha was worried.

She wiggled her way across the snow to her husband's side. With stubborn determination, she got the gag off and began working on the rope around her wrists, using her teeth.

The ropes were not especially tight. She was making progress.

Fifty minutes had passed since the horse had whinnied to announce the approach of the two men. The ropes finally off her hands, she gathered her husband into her arms, brushing the snow off his face. She kissed his mouth and tried to warm his cold face.

The blankets that had been wrapped around them had come with Holmes as he was dragged into the pit. They lay a few feet away. She removed her red hat and laid it under her husband's cheek. Crawling, she retrieved the blankets and wrapped them around him. She tried unsuccessfully to unfasten the ropes around her ankles but gave it up. Her fingers were too cold.

Samantha Louise Johnson pulled John Holmes' head onto her lap, replaced the hat on her head, and pulled one blanket down around their ankles, the other over their heads.

At 11:00 p.m. Olsen Farmer looked outside again for the third time. No dad. He called the residence. No answer.

The two brothers exchanged looks.

"Something is wrong, Phillip. They wouldn't stay out in this storm for four hours."

"Let's go," said Phillip.

They walked in the beauty of new snow following the nearly invisible sleigh tracks. They both carried lanterns. One set of tracks led across the new bridge, with no sign of a returning set.

The resolute teenagers headed for the door of the staff apartments. Their pounding woke up Kendall Wiles in the nearest cabin. When he opened his door, Phillip ran over to explain.

Jon Davis opened the door angrily, annoyed at being awakened but the anguished faces of the Farmer boys drove the feeling away.

Dressed warmly, the four followed the sleigh marks across the bridge.

Jenny Davis hurried into the main house and woke Carrie and I.

I followed the other four men in a jeep equipped with tire chains. Ian Reilly accompanied me. Sue and Washington Foster went to the house to be with Carrie, Jenny, and the children.

My heart filled with apprehension, I stopped so suddenly that I skidded into the back of the empty sleigh but did no damage.

The tracks were nearly obliterated by the freshly deposited flakes but it was not hard to figure out that something extraordinary had happened here.

While Olsen and Phillip Farmer walked south following what they thought were footprints, Ian and I walked along the top of the pit, shinning our lights into it. In the center we could see the pile of earth covered with snow.

I tripped on something in the thick white stuff.

"Are you all right, Patrick?"

"Yes, I tripped on something buried…in the snow." My voice quivered. I dropped to the ground and began to brush away snow. Ian followed my example.

Our efforts revealed a rough wooden plank. I breathed in cold air and sighed in relief.

A sound startled me. It was like the wind but there was no wind.

"Ian, did you hear…?"

"Yes, sir. From the pit I think."

We stared at the pile of dirt in the center as it began to move. Snow tumbled down its slope to reveal a red hat and then a frightened face.

"Kendall, here. Hurry!"

"The plank, sir."

Three of us ran down the board. Falling to my knees, I grabbed Samantha and hugged her to me. Kendall removed the blankets and brushed snow off my brother. His eyes opened.

"Are you hurt?"

Holmes shook his head no.

"How about you, Samantha?"

"No, Patrick. But my ankles are tied."

A surge of anger swept over me. I kissed her forehead while Kendall cut the offending ropes with a pocketknife. I picked her up and carried her up the boardwalk, Kendall and Ian on either side of me to steady my ascent. I put her in the jeep and ran back to help with Holmes.

Holmes was taller and heavier than any of us. We put him on Ian's back, arms wrapped around the man's neck. Holmes held on to Ian, Ian held John Holmes' arms. Kendall followed behind Ian, partially attempting to carry some of the injured man's weight. I walked beside the plank, steadying their climb. We got him at last into the jeep.

"We are troubled on every side," mumbled Holmes, "yet not dis…"

His words slurred.

I supplied the word, "distressed."

"We are perplexed, but not in despair; persecuted, but not forsaken; cast down…" my brother's voice broke.

I finished the verse for him. "Cast down, but not destroyed. That is from I Corinthians 4, verses 8 and 9."

"You are both safe now, Holmes," said Ian Reilly. He climbed in the jeep.

Just as I started the engine, there was a cry from Phillip. Kendall took off running. "You go on, Patrick. We can follow in the sleigh. Go with him, Ian, he will need your help."

It was 2:00 o'clock in the morning before we had the three in their respective beds.

Except for a bruise on John Holmes' forehead and a knot on Olsen's, there were no injuries.

Because of the ropes, Owen's fingertips and Samantha's toes were on the verge of frostbite.

We called Doctor Ron.

*****

In the early hours of the morning, Friday January 15, J.B. Hobert and his son, Lloyd, were attacked in their home. Cal was not at the house. Nevin and Faxon were in a cell at the Kansas City, Missouri Police Station, pending bail being set by a Judge.

There would be no breakfast at Judy's Café.

As a quiet dream
A field of Marshmallow white
Stretches far across the map
Shrouding the world in silence
Charmingly peaceful

Chapter eleven

Day Dreamer
January 15-20, 1943

I called my brother-in-law at 8:00 o'clock Friday morning.

"Patrick here, Joel. You are not going to believe this. It's about Holmes and Samantha."

I finished my explanation and waited for the reaction.

"Patrick, are they hurt? They are going to be all right?"

"Relax, Joel. Joseph says they are fine, just cold and tired. They will sleep a lot for the next two days. Holmes asked me to convey his apology about breakfast. He wants to know if you could come to the residence for lunch instead, say at 1:00? It's important."

"At 1:00 o'clock?"

"Yes. I'm going to call the clinic and cancel his therapy session."

"Right. One it is. I will call the others so you won't have to.

Thanks, Patrick, for calling so promptly. I am relieved they are all right."

I stayed home from work to help out. Carrie and I went to the residence at eleven to assist Sue Foster as she prepared for five guests. We let Holmes sleep until the company arrived.

When the doorbell rang my wife and I met Joel and the other detectives in the entryway. Joel made introductions.

"My sister-in-law, Carrie Overly and her husband, Patrick Overly. Patrick and Holmes are foster brothers. I'd like you to meet two Detectives from Kansas City, Kansas, Charlie Raymond and Innes Wallace. This is Detective Robert Wright of the KCMO PD. Zeke is on the way."

Everyone greeted everyone else. All the coats were hung up; boots were lined up on a rug.

"How are they, Mr. Overly?"

"Still asleep, Detective Raymond. I will go get Holmes now. Carrie will show you to the dining room."

Fifteen minutes later I wheeled my brother into the room, still in his pajamas and wearing a thick bathrobe. His face and hands were red and blotched from the long exposure to the snow and there was one bruise on his forehead. He looked tired despite his long sleep. His eyes had the haunted look that I was well acquainted with.

At the table sat five men. Zeke Martin had arrived in my absence. My brother stared blankly at the flowers in the center of the table. Sue Foster stood at the door between kitchen and dining area; Carrie stood behind me with her hands on my shoulders.

I touched John Holmes' arm. "What is it, Holmes?"

He actually jerked in his chair, that far away had his mind been from his present situation.

"I am sorry. Was I day-dreaming?"

"Yes, Holmes. You have company." I said it gently. I already knew what was troubling him. "Samantha and the baby are all right. Owen just has a bump on the head, as do you."

He seemed to be looking through me.

"Did you hear me?"

"Yes. My wife and baby are all right, Owen is well." He finally looked at me, and than at the other men in the room with total awareness. "It was the Juarez brothers."

"Yes," said Charlie.

"They tied her up." He closed his eyes for a second. When he opened them, they flashed with anger. "They tied up my wife and dragged me around in the snow like a child's toy."

"We know that. You are safe and warm again, my friend." Joel sounded extremely solemn until he added; "Can we eat now?"

John Holmes Johnson began to laugh.

Sue and Carrie served lunch.

Samantha came up behind Holmes and put her arms around his neck.

"My wife, gentlemen, Samantha Louise Johnson…"

She moved to the side of the chair and lifted his hand to her stomach.

"And son," he finished proudly.

Everyone was eating Quiche Lorraine with obvious pleasure when Holmes spoke again.

"Remember when we talked to Sandra Rose, Robert? She said that one of the kidnappers kept referring to her as, "'Little lady.'" He took a bite and then another.

Robert Wright ate the last scrap of the cheesy treat before responding. "Yes, I remember. Why?"

"Juan Juarez said and I quote, "'You will do as I say or the little lady is dead.'" Later he said it again."

"John was face down in the snow with the man's boot on his back." Samantha kissed him. "Poor darling."

Sue Foster brought in cups of pudding, distributing them as Carrie removed empty plates.

Detective Wright emptied his coffee cup. "Same man, you think?"

"Holmes shrugged. "Very possible. I sent an inquiry to Mexico City. I received this response. It came in Wednesday's mail." He handed the letter to Charlie Raymond.

Eyebrow up, Charlie removed the paper from its envelope and read aloud.

"In answer to your query, señor, a señora Cynthia Barrett Alexander Bartlett and son, Robert Brian, did indeed move to Mexico in 1909. She divorced her American husband and in 1911 she remarried. The husband, Juan Juarez, was a prominent businessman in Mexico City. Both died in 1930.

The couple had one son, Eduardo Raol Juarez. Robert was adopted and renamed, Juan Roberto Juarez." Charlie looked up and whistled.

"So," said Innes, "we have a direct connection from the old Alexander Construction Company to the present attack on Holmes."

"Quite right," I said.

There were chuckles around the table.

I felt myself blushing.

"Telephone call for Detective Raymond, Mr. Johnson."

"Thank you, Sue."

Charlie stood up.

"Follow me, sir."

He returned five minutes later looking quite somber. He sat down and finished his pudding.

"We must go, Holmes. J.B. Hobert is dead. His son, Lloyd, in critical condition at Bethany Hospital."

Sue suddenly appeared at the door, breathless. "Mr. Johnson, it's Marian on the telephone, sir."

Joel pushed the chair to the phone, followed by a procession of five men and two women.

Holmes addressed Marian apprehensively, but a moment later his grin told us what we all wanted to hear. "Malcolm and George are awake. George asked Georganne to marry him and Malcolm asked for food."

Samantha sat on her husband's lap and they hugged. She kissed the bruised forehead.

There were a few minutes of jubilation and handshaking before Holmes finished his message. "George wants to see you and Zeke, Joel. I'll go with you."

"No way. You are to go back to bed. Doctor's orders."

"But, Patrick..."

"No!"

"Carrie?"

She shook her head emphatically.

"Come on, Joel, help me out here."

"Sorry, Holmes. I agree with Carrie. Besides, I can't go against my sister-in-law. My wife would kill me."

Holmes chuckled at first but laughed heartily when Samantha poked her cousin by marriage and said, "You got that right, mister."

After everyone had left, Carrie and I saw the couple back to bed and then I went back to the Overly plant to put in a few hours of work.

I did not return home until 7:30 p.m. My family had waited for me so we were eating at 8:00 when the next telephone call came.

Lloyd Brock Hobert had died at 7:09 following his father in death by a few hours.

Saturday was low-key and gray. Holmes and Samantha napped off and on all morning. At 1:00 o'clock, I drove them into Kansas City to visit George and Malcolm. Marian returned with us, at the urging of her husband.

Malcolm was irate over the attack on his boss and even threatened to check himself out of the hospital in total disregard for the advice of his doctor.

Holmes succeeded in talking him out of it.

George and Georganne discussed their marriage plans.

On the way back to the estate it began to spit snow.

Sunday morning we awoke to a white world that stretched out in all directions from our large two-story house. The cabins were nearly buried with tall wind-whipped drifts half way up the doors. The wooden walkway was under three feet of a thick white quilt. It was gorgeous.

No one from the estate made it to church. It took us hours just to dig ourselves out.

There was no school Monday. Seven Midwest states were inundated by a massive snowstorm that swept across the middle of the United States. States from Colorado to Indiana, plus Iowa and Ohio, were covered.

By mid-morning Tuesday, all major thoroughfares were cleared and many secondary roads were at least passable. The two Kansas Cities began to stir like two huge hibernating polar bears.

The car the Juarez brothers had left town in was found in a ditch off highway 69, twenty miles north of El Dorado, Kansas. No trace of the men.

Sandra Rose went back to her home.

Wednesday, Malcolm was released from the hospital. William Leonard drove him to the estate.

George was given a one-month leave of absence and left town with his fiancée and her family. The couple would return February 18 as Mr. and Mrs. George St. Giles.

Ice crystals collide
Attach to their own kind
Create exquisite dancers
A natural bombardment
Of soft falling snow

Chapter twelve

The Blizzard
January 14-18, 1943

On Thursday night, the attack was swift.

The moonlit snow, which had been so romantically beautiful minutes before, now assumed an eerie spookiness.

Juan glanced at his watch. "8:20," he muttered aloud.

Holmes tried to move his face out of the snow but the man's boot pressed down on him even harder. There was a short cry from the pit.

Seconds dragged. Just as Holmes got his left arm free from underneath his own body and grabbed the sneering man's ankle, he was jerked violently away.

A gloating Eduardo pulled him by the ankles through the snow and down the board plank that served as a ramp.

The man slipped, sitting down abruptly. Cursing, he made it to his feet, kicking the snow from the board as though to revenge himself on the unfeeling white stuff that had so embarrassed him.

Holmes held onto the plank with a stubborn determination to resist.

Juan stomped his left hand.

Once in the deep hole, the brothers set their victim on his feet and turned him toward the center where he saw his wife, bound and gagged. She was leaning against a mound of snow-covered dirt.

"Samant…"

It was as far as he got before a fist slammed into his stomach.

"You should not have gotten involved, Señor Johnson. Enjoy your stay here."

With a laugh to indicate his pleasure, the seemingly speechless Eduardo gripped John Holmes' shoulders and shoved him with all his might.

Holmes landed face down in the wet stuff, his forehead struck the frozen dirt pile. He was dazed.

"Adios."

So, he does talk, thought the groggy man. He giggled slightly just before Eduardo's boot landed on his back. He passed out.

Samantha watched the two men disappear over the brink and then she watched in horrified concentration as the 12"x2" wooden escape route was pulled up. She tried to squeeze back tears as she listened to the crunch of retreating footsteps.

Juan and his brother walked south through the trees dragging tree branches to obscure their tracks. With luck the falling snow would cover up the roughened path before rescuers arrived.

After a twenty-minute walk, they stepped out of the woods onto a narrow road and climbed into a truck, its flat bed loaded with lumber and sacks of sand for weight.

Juan drove slowly west toward State Line Road.

"Now we will eliminate J.B. Hobert and go home. How about that, Eduardo?"

"Si, mi hermano. I miss my girl friends. I would like to have a fire, some tequila, and Rosita," he paused, "or Marguarita, or Louisa…" he shrugged. "It doesn't matter."

Juan laughed at his younger brother. "When we get home to our hacienda, we will have a fiesta muy grande. You can have all the tequila and all the girls you want, little brother." He slapped his brother's shoulder.

"What will you do?"

"I think I will marry Miguela and have a bunch of urchins. I will name the girls Roberta and the boys Roberto."

"All of them?"

"Si. All of them."

The brothers laughed merrily.

Juan turned off State Line Road. Eventually he was heading west on highway 32 toward the Hobert home in Edwardsville.

There was little traffic so he made good, if somewhat slow, progress.

At 10:45 p.m. he pulled the truck onto the grounds of the J.B. Construction lot and hid the truck.

After donning hats and gloves, the two men left the vehicle and stepped into the thick underbrush and weeds that lined the southern edge of the lot, separating it from the railroad tracks that ran east and west for miles and miles.

In front of them, approximately a thousand feet away, was the two-story, one hundred-year-old house of the Hobert family. Behind them was a truck with a yellow cab, a black flatbed, a broken headlight, and smears of paint from a black Ford.

The brothers glanced back at the row of seven trucks, all with yellow cabs and black flatbeds, parked in a large area littered with many kinds of construction equipment; caterpillars, cement mixers, a back hoe, a bulldozer, and a half-dozen pickup trucks.

They moved on. They approached the house and looked around from the cover of the trees. The huge house sat at an angle, its front door facing NE and Highway 32. Behind the house, sitting perpendicular to it, was a long carport.

"Four cars," said Juan. "That's Lloyd's, J.B.'s, Nevin's, and Faxon's. good. That means Cal is not home. Perfect."

"Now?"

"Now would be good."

Eduardo took a slingshot and a small rock from his pocket and shot out the light on the back porch.

The two crouched low and waited.

No one came to the door to investigate the noise. They moved up to the carport.

Juan pointed to a lighted, first-floor room. "J.B. is in his study."

"How do you know this?"

"I've been in the house before, little brother." He pointed up. "Lloyd is in his bedroom."

A second light came on. "Now he is in his bathroom." He laughed quietly. "This is great."

"Let's move. I'm cold." Eduardo shivered.

"Go."

They ran to the now-darkened porch. In seconds Juan had it open with a key from his ring of stolen keys.

The house was warm. The two stood still for ten minutes, rubbing cold hands.

Juan touched his brother's arm and pointed. The two moved cautiously toward the lighted study. Peeking around the doorframe, Juan could see J.B. sitting at his desk in the center of the room.

The study had two doors. One opened into the long main hallway, while the one Juan stood in opened into a short hall leading to a bathroom. Two large mahogany desks faced each other in the center. Two smaller roll-tops sat against the north wall. The unsuspecting man had his back to Juan Juarez, his account books open in front of him.

The brothers stepped in and closed the distance between them and the seated man in less time than it took J.B. Hobert to react to the small clink of metal against wood that he heard behind him.

Two men swung metal rods simultaneously, striking the man on both sides of his head. He died instantly from the blow to his right temple.

J.B. slumped forward, bloodied head on his desk pad.

Juan hit him again for good measure. He laid the metal rod by the body and dropped a sheet of sandpaper on the floor. With a jerk of his head, he led his brother to the staircase that led up to the five bedrooms.

When Lloyd Brice Hobert switched off the light and stepped out of his bathroom, he was felled by a blow to the back of his neck. Another blow struck him even as he fell forward, face down on a blue and green plaid throw rug. He did not hear the loud sound of the metal weapon hitting the floor or the evil cackle of his assailants.

Eduardo threw the sandpaper down. It landed on Lloyd's back.

"Let's get out before Cal comes home."

Juan picked up a set of car keys from the night table. "Un momento, Eduardo. Follow me." He went into a different bedroom. Taking down a picture to reveal a safe, he pointed. "Search the room for anything we can steal, little brother. I'll see if I can open this safe."

At 11:12 p.m. Thursday night, the two left by the same door they had entered and drove away in Lloyd's car. It had taken less then seventeen minutes to kill two men and steal over $2000.

*****

It would be 2:00 o'clock Friday afternoon before Cal Brent arrived home and discovered the grisly scene. At 2:30, the message reached Detective Charlie Raymond at the Johnson Residence.

J.B. Hobert had adamantly refused police protection, now he was dead.

Juan drove to a small diner at the intersection of Leavenworth Road and Seven highway where they had left their car. While Juan started it to warm it up, Eduardo went in the diner to buy sandwiches and coffee.

It was past midnight. The snow was falling relentlessly, the drive from the Hobert home in Edwardsville to the diner had taken nearly an hour, now road conditions were far worse. Nibbling on his ham sandwich, Juan cautiously pulled onto the highway headed south for Olathe and then he went south on 69. He drove for hours through blowing snow with visibility becoming increasingly difficult. Twenty miles outside of El Dorado, Kansas, something darted into the slick road in front of their car. He tried to avoid contact, skidded, struck the deer a glancing blow, and went off the road. The car slid sideways into several trees and stopped.

"What was that?" asked a shaken Eduardo.

"Deer, I think."

The brothers tried but could not free the car from its snowy prison. Juan turned off the engine with its distinctive ping. The silence seemed as solid as the snow covered tree they were trapped against.

"Map," said Juan suddenly.

"We are about here. Have to walk, brother. Let's eat those last two sandwiches. Then we'll put on extra socks and sweaters before we start walking."

"What if we get lost?"

"If we stick to the highway, maybe we can get a ride."

Eduardo laughed. "Who would be stupid enough to be out in this blizzard?"

Juan looked at his brother fondly. The two laughed so hard that the car rocked, dumping snow from the roof.

After raiding their suitcases and putting on extra clothes, they stuffed their pockets with things they did not want to leave behind. They set out for the nearest town.

*****

By 4:00 p.m. Charlie Raymond was sitting at a kitchen table across from a distraught Cal Hobert. "Where were you, Cal?"

The man took his hands away from his face and stared at the coffee cup. He picked it up and drained it. Finally he looked up at the detective.

"What did you say?"

"I need to know where you were."

"Of course." The voice sounded mechanical, drained of feeling.

He let out a long, ragged breath before speaking. "I left Edwardsville at 3:00 o'clock Thursday. I drove to Salina, Kansas to bid on a job. By 6:30 it was snowing heavily. I got a room in a Best Western. I ate a quick breakfast Friday morning and started for home." He shook his head and pressed his hands against both sides as though to keep it in its proper place. "The highway was terrible. It took me seven hours to reach Edwardsville. I shouldn't have spent the night. Maybe my being here would have made a difference." His eyes looked pain-filled and anguished.

"And then again, maybe not," said Charlie. "We might be investigating an attack on three victims. Don't blame yourself, son. I tried to post a police guard but your father refused." Charlie stared at his cup just as Cal had done minutes before.

"Not your fault, sir. My father was a stubborn man."

Innes Wallace entered the room. "Just had a call from the lab boys. Guess whose prints were on the handbrake of Malcolm Macdougal's car?"

"Juan Juarez' perhaps?"

Innes nodded. "That's not all. They also found different prints on the light switch and basement door at Lucille Sloan's house. Also from Juan Juarez."

Charlie stood up. "If you feel like coming downtown, Cal, we will turn your two brother's loose into your custody. You three will have plans to make and details to work out."

Cal stood up. "Thank you."

"I hope your brother makes it."

The three brothers reached their home but it seemed foreign to them. The study and staircase to the second floor were closed off with yellow police tape and an officer was spending the night.

"I don't think I could sleep here anyway, Cal" said Nevin, tears rolling from both eyes.

"Nor I, big brother. I'll call Abigail, and see if we can spend the night there." Faxon looked at his older brother a second before he added; "I have asked her to marry me."

"Good for you. I expect you both to get married. I want to be an uncle."

The telephone rang at 7:14 before Faxon could pick it up.

Faxon dropped the phone as though it had suddenly gotten too hot to hold. He stared at it, speechless.

"What is it?"

"Lloyd died at 7:09."

"That's impossible," yelled Nevin. "They said he was doing better. They said he was going to make it." Nevin sat down in the nearest chair. "This can't be happening."

Cal looked out the window at the snow. "Maybe the blizzard

will blow itself out." His wistful voice choked and the room was silent except for the soft sobs of Nevin Hobert.

*****

January 18 the mail brought my brother news from England. It was from a family friend, Michael Jonus, now 49 and a music teacher. In 1904, Jonus had become head of the infamous Baker Street irregulars after the young Mr. Wiggins was stabbed to death. He had lived and worked with Doctor John Watson and the two had become as father and son. The house at 221 Baker Street had passed to him. The Haven that Inspector Lestrade and Doctor Watson had opened on Oxford Street to help the homeless children of London was now a pile of rubble. The house at 221 B had been damaged in the incessant bombing of London but the Jonus family was still able to occupy it.

Jonus and Alicia lived on the ground floor, once occupied by the indomitable Emma Hudson and renters lived upstairs. Living space was at a premium these days in the battered city.

John Holmes read what Jonus had written; "Christmas 1942 was sparse for Great Britain. Shops were crowded but there was very little to be purchased. Toys were nearly unobtainable. Food was scarce and it was illegal to give away your food stamps as gifts to friends and loved ones.

"England's proud people began to make appeals in the newspapers for used toys and clothes and perhaps for the first time, many did not mind wearing some one else's hand-me-downs.

"Theaters are presenting plays by Shakespeare, Bernard Shaw, and Oscar Wilde. People are returning to London and repairing their homes.

"There is a waiting list for flats. Hotels, restaurants, and taxis operate a steady business. All of this despite the constant threat of renewed attacks.

"The week of Christmas there was a 'Potato Christmas Fair' sponsored by the Ministry of Food. It was held in the bombed out shell of an Oxford street store. Quite fun.

"Here is a bit of news; the Home Guard began admitting women, as a constant vigilance must be maintained against the threat of German attack and invasion.

"U-boats continue to bombard the shipping lanes making even so common a commodity as bread, expensive and hard to obtain."

John Holmes looked up from the letter at a sob from Sean Douglas, not too distantly removed from the horrors of war-torn London. Colin put his arm around his twin brother.

Sean got to his feet and went to his adoptive mother, Jenny Davis.

She hugged his curly head to her.

"I am sorry, mother."

"For what, darling?"

"For throwing away my crust, for not eating what you provide for me, for forgetting." He sobbed on her shoulder. "We were there, Colin and me. How could I forget so soon?"

Jenny kissed the ten-year-old boy's forehead. "It's all right, Sean. We all must do better. We are all guilty of squandering our blessings." She raised his face and looked into his sad eyes. "I love you, Sean Douglas."

Colin walked over to stand beside her and she put her other arm around him.

"Davis, mother. We want to be Sean and Colin Davis. Can we do that?"

Jenny Davis could only cry.

Jon Davis answered for his wife. "I will find out, Colin. I think it is a distinct possibility. Holmes?"

"Indeed so. Should not be hard to find out. I shall inquire of Edgar Vernon."

Sean sat down on the sofa next to his mother and in typical young man fashion wiped his eyes and nose on his sleeve. Jon Davis pressed a handkerchief into his hand.

Sanford and Hudson climbed onto John Holmes' lap. Sanford wrapped his three-year-old arms around the man and hugged him.

Sean grinned.

Four close families sat quietly in my drawing room for a few minutes and I remembered the words of the hymn, 'Count your blessings, name them one by one and it will surprise you what the Lord has done'.

"Is there more, callan?"

Holmes nodded at Malcolm's question. "Aye, a lot more."

Samantha gave her husband a quick kiss before he began to read again.

"Captain Samuel Hilliary and his son Shane live with us. Samuel married our daughter Joanna. She died fourteen days later. Shane is as priceless to us as if he were our own grandson.

"I am working in a factory producing warplanes. There is little work for a music teacher right now. Music is in demand however. To that end, a group of us present weekly free concerts. Times are hard but not unbearable.

"One last note, John Holmes. Before he died, Leslie Oakshott asked me to look after his damaged property in Surrey. He told me he was leaving it to you and arranged to pay me a monthly salary to maintain it. With your approval, I have engaged a person of your acquaintance to live in the house and watch over it, John Gregson, now retired from Scotland Yard and his wife, Adadira. He is 77 but healthy and still a formidable opponent when challenged. I would appreciate your reply. Mail is getting through fairly well considering the circumstances. Your friend and servant, Michael Jonus."

The room was very quiet.

We were warm and comfortable, surrounded by the cheerful fire, the ticking clock, and a mantle of love. Our hardships in America seemed infinitesimally small when compared to the nearly unbearable struggles of the people in war ravaged Europe. And not only Europe. The peoples of Africa, Asia, Australia, and all over the South Pacific were suffering. There was no place safe from this war. The world was bleeding.

In predator style
Go after the weakest link
Turn brother against brother
Eliminate the leader
Destroy confidence

Chapter thirteen

One Family
January 19, 1943

It was a postcard, picture-perfect day. An unbroken field of white greeted us when we woke up on the nineteenth. The sky was blue. The air clear, cold, and fresh.

Three inches of new snow covered the walk and the driveway.

Both our households were slow to stir from the warmth and comfort of thick quilts. Carrie and I snuggled in our bed, thankful for the simple fact that no bombs would suddenly shatter the peace and smash our home.

I dozed off. In a kind of slow motion movie, I watched windows blow out noiselessly, the ceiling fall by chunks, and then a bookcase fell over with a loud thud. I was startled awake by the noise followed by the wails of Lori Marie.

I was out of bed in an instant.

Lori Marie had tripped and fallen onto her dollhouse. The

roof had collapsed, knocking over the tiny furniture and burying the two minuscule dolls that lived there.

I hugged my small daughter to me as I surveyed the damage.

"It will be all right, Lori. Daddy can fix it, wait and see."

Carrie entered and picked up our daughter.

I carefully lifted the roof off the wooden house and set it aside. "Look here, Lori. Nothing is broken, honey."

The two tiny dolls were snuggled in bed just as we had been and the heavy roof had not touched them. I helped my daughter set up the fallen furniture and replace the tiny books on shelves.

Lori peeked under the miniature blanket and decided that Fred and Rita were all right. She tenderly tucked the blanket around them and placed the tiny dog on the foot of the bed.

With a huge grin, she threw her arms around my neck and kissed me.

"Thank you, daddy. I love you."

There was a loud sound from the nursery so Carrie headed that way.

At 9:15, a parade of hungry Overlys went down the spiral staircase. I carried Hannah. Sanford and Hudson led the way exuberantly, followed closely by Lori, then Carrie, and then Hannah and I. Jenny and her boys met us at the foot of the steps.

Sanford ran to Sean, Hudson jumped into Colin's arms, and Lori Marie raised her arms to Jenny who dutifully lifted her up and kissed her strawberry birthmark.

Lori giggled as Jenny tickled her neck but then she got very serious.

"Daddy?"

"What, darling?"

"I want to see Owen today. He needs to kiss my mark of an angel for good luck. I want to see him, daddy."

"All right, Lori. I'll invite them to lunch. How about that?"

"Oh goody, goody."

She wiggled out of Jenny's arms and headed for the breakfast nook.

Jenny took Hannah Elisabeth and followed the children. I took my wife into my arms.

When we made it to the table, all six children were involved with bowls of oatmeal and hot biscuits with honey.

*****

In the residence, Marian followed the wheelchair that her husband temporarily occupied. He was suffering some disorientation and dizziness because of damage to the right ear. When he stood up, his head swam crazily and he was unable to keep his balance.

Malcolm knocked at the door of the master bedroom and waited for Samantha to answer. Before Holmes married, he would have sailed right in and helped his boss toilet and dress. Now, he always knocked first.

The door opened and a fully dressed Samantha stood to one side while the Scotsman wheeled through. The two women hugged.

Holmes sat on the edge of the bed buttoning a light blue shirt, a task that was becoming increasingly easier. The fingers of his right hand were working stiffly, but at last resuming some of their function. The arm still needed help getting where it was needed but even that was improving.

Malcolm watched his boss struggle with the button next to the top.

"Dinna ye need a wee bit of help, callan?"

There was something in the voice that stayed John Holmes' stubborn no. He looked into the mottled face and hazel eyes of his countryman a second, reading the anguish there.

"Aye, ye dour Scotsman. I thought ye wad never get back tae work."

Soberly, Malcolm Macdougal fastened the stubborn button that gave even him some trouble, so small was it.

"I thought I wad surely dee."

John Holmes reached out. Malcolm took his hand into his own two large ones, and then squeezed it gently.

Their eyes met.

"I understand, my friend."

"Awell, breakfast syne, laddie. I am vera hungry." He backed his wheelchair up and sat watching Samantha help her husband with his trousers.

Marian's arms went around her husband's neck. Kissing the top of his head on his short cropped hair, she said, "Come help me, lo'e?"

Twenty minutes later the four sat at the table with poached eggs, biscuits and jelly.

The distinct scraping sound of a snow shovel filtered into the dining room.

"More snow last night?" asked Holmes around his coffee cup.

Marian went to the window. "Aye, looks like three inches or so. Kendall has shoveled all the way to the porch. Shall I invite him in for coffee?"

"Great idea," said Samantha even as her husband said, "Indeed so."

In seconds, an obviously cold Kendall Wiles sat at the table with rosy cheeks, cradling the warm cup between his red, work roughened hands.

"Tastes wonderful."

"Have a biscuit, Kendall." Marian put two on a plate in front of him.

"Have some jelly," said Samantha.

"Wad ye like an egg, lad?"

"No, thank you." He looked from face to face. "What is this? Are you planning to fire me and you are softening the blow?" He grinned but it faded fast as no one immediately spoke.

Holmes cleared his throat. "On the contrary, Kendall. If you have a twin, I would very much like to hire him also. Do you?"

"Sorry, sir. I am one of a kind."

"A raise then?"

Kendall shook his head, as he said, "No," emphatically. "No, Holmes, I don't need a raise. I don't need anything. I have a nice place to live, a job I like, and friends-I don't need anything else." He shrugged, "Maybe a wife." He chuckled.

Malcolm offered his hand. "Thank ye, callan. Because ye wer heir for tham, I dow could git hale. I didna fash, knowing ye were heir. Thank ye, lad."

"My pleasure, Malcolm. I like these folks as much as you do."

Marian kissed his cheek and the 47-year-old groundskeeper blushed like a teenager.

"Any prospects?" asked Samantha.

The man looked perplexed.

"For a wife," Samantha added.

"Well…maybe." He blushed again.

"You have a girl, Kendall? That is excellent. You must bring her around." Picking up his cup, Holmes added, "Quite right," for good measure. "Blast it." He sat the empty cup down.

Laughing at her husband's expression, Samantha refilled it and then capped off everyone's cup.

"What's her name, callan…unless ye wad rather nae say."

"No, it's all right. I haven't said anything to anyone. I was afraid it wouldn't last, you know." The big man actually sighed rather wistfully. "Her name is Wilma Lilias. She is 46, widowed, no children. Lives at Lake Quivera in Kansas and works for a doctor and his family. She loves the outdoors as much as I do."

He paused as though deciding how much to say. "She knew your parents, Samantha."

"How?"

"In 1917, she was twenty, you were ten. She lived two blocks from your folks and baby-sat with you. She was there that night…"

"When the accident happened." Samantha sucked in a deep breath and held her husband's left arm tightly. "I remember her. Wilma Randolph. I called her Willa." Her eyes misted.

Kendall looked flustered. "I am so sorry. I have upset you." He stood up. "I need to get back to work. I need to clear the porch and the deck."

"It's quite all right, Kendall. I would love to see Willa again. Please ask her to come visit, perhaps next weekend for dinner. At least ask her."

"Yes, ma'am. I'll do that. I need her to meet you all and see my cabin. I know she will love the estate, the grounds and the lake. Excuse me and thank you for the coffee and biscuits."

As he passed the Scotsman, he said, "Glad you are back with us, Malcolm."

"And I am a sonsy mon to be hame noo."

Marian walked him to the door.

"What exciting news, I can hardly wait to see Willa, darling."

"Why do ye call the lass, Willa?"

Samantha giggled. "She was always reading, 'O Pioneer!' by Willa Cather. She could quote whole passages."

Marian announced a phone call for Holmes. As Samantha pushed her husband out of the room, the couple heard dishes tinkling, the squeak of a chair, and then a resounding kiss. Samantha stifled a chuckle as she headed down the hall.

She greeted her cousin by marriage. "Good morning, Joel. Are you keeping my cousin warm?"

A chuckle preceded his affirmative comment. "As a matter of fact, we are still in bed, all cozy and comfy."

Samantha heard a giggle and then a slap on bare skin. "We are not," said Adele, "in bed, we are on the bed. Talk to you when the guys are done, okay?"

"All right, darling. Put Joel back on."

She handed the telephone over to Holmes, giving instructions with a kiss.

"Got it. When I am finished do not hang up."

"Now don't forget."

"Quite right. Do not forget. Got it!"

Blowing a kiss, she disappeared down the hall toward the kitchen.

"Joel?"

"About time, old chap. I have implicit instructions not to hang up when we are finished. Remind me."

Holmes laughed. "Same here. I'll be the one to forget, no doubt."

"I've got some news, Holmes. Kansas City, Kansas police found the hit and run truck. And State police in Liberal, Kansas rescued two nearly frozen men from a snow bank off Highway 54 about an hour ago. Guess who?"

"Our murderers I hope."

"The Juarez brothers were forty miles from the Texas border. They had abandoned Lloyd's car at Victory Diner on Highway 7 and made it almost to El Dorado, Kansas before they slid off the road. Can you believe they walked to town in that blizzard?"

"Indeed. They were, after all, highly motivated."

Joel laughed. "Didn't think of it that way. You are right, Holmes. They bought a car with the money stolen from the Hobert safe, equipped it with chains, loaded up with bags of sand, snow shovels and food, and then left town. They made it to Liberal."

"Skillful driving. What stopped them?"

Chuckling at the question, Joel answered cheerfully. "Ran out of gas. They couldn't find any stations open so they decided to risk making it to the first town over the Oklahoma border. They planned to hole up there but never made it. They were pretty frozen by the time they were discovered."

"When are you planning to go pick them up? Or is Detective Raymond and his partner going for them?"

"Actually, in an unprecedented act of cooperation between KCK and KCMO police departments, we are both going as soon as the weather clears and the roads are reasonably safe to travel. Juan and Eduardo are under a doctor's care for exposure and dehydration."

"Dehydration?"

"Since they were out of gas, there was no heat. No heat caused the doors and windows to freeze shut. They couldn't get to the snow without breaking a window. If they did that, they would freeze to death." Joel laughed ruefully. "They were actually glad to see the police."

"The brothers killed five people, assuming of course, that they killed Eric and Lucille as well as the Judge, and the two Hobert men."

"They also assaulted six others with intent to kill. Dangerous men, my friend."

"Absolutely."

"I'll keep you posted, Holmes. Stay warm."

"I will try."

"Don't hang up, Holmes," yelled Joel Anderson. "My wife won't feed me lunch."

John Holmes laughed.

"We are finished, Samantha."

"I'm right here, darling." She relieved him of the phone and sat down on the phone bench.

Marian stood nearby quietly watching her boss, gamely,

with great effort, turning the wheelchair. Facing her, he grinned charmingly and pushed his brown peppered with gray, quite attractive hair away from his forehead.

"Hi, Marian."

She laughed at his boyish tone. "Where to, boss?"

"Library please. Where is Malcolm?"

"In the kitchen making egg noodles for dinner. Do you want him?"

"When he is finished. There's no hurry."

When Marian returned minutes later with tea, Holmes was writing a letter to Michael Jonus.

*****

At 12:15, Samantha leaned on the library door and folded her arms. "We are invited to the main house for lunch at one. Owen and the boys will be there. Do you mind?"

"I am delighted. I haven't seen Owen or the boys since the sleigh ride." Her husband looked at the letter in his hand. "I have not had the opportunity to thank Olsen and Phillip personally for coming after us. We could very well have frozen to death."

She walked in to sit on his lap. "I know, darling."

Marian found them sitting in the library, foreheads touching, and arms around each other. She coughed before she spoke. "Time to get coats on. Patrick and Davis are here to help us."

"Good news. Thank you, Marian."

Samantha started to rise from her seat. Marian gave her a hand up and then left the room.

"I love you, Samantha Louise."

"Come on you two," I said as I entered the library. "Malcolm is bundled up like an Eskimo. Your turn, Holmes."

"Lunch better be worth braving the snow, Patrick. Of course, the company will make up for any deficiencies in the meal." He chuckled. "Don't tell Janis I said that."

"That you questioned her ability to provide a delicious lunch. Would I do that?"

On the walkway, Samantha kept a tight grip on the rail not wishing to risk a fall with a baby due in March. Marian walked beside her.

Owen Farmer met the wheelchair in mid-room. Owen pulled Holmes to his feet and the two men hugged. It was the second time that the two men had been in peril of their lives together.

"Owen, you are recovered?"

"Yes. I just had a bump on my hard head. My toes got mighty cold."

"I am so sorry, Owen."

"Be quiet, sir. It weren't something we could of predicted, now were it? Well, get over here boys, and greet John Holmes."

Still standing up with Owen's support, Holmes hugged the two young teens. Samantha joined them for a three-way hug.

Phillip held Samantha's wrist and gallantly kissed the bruises made by the rope as she labored to remove it with her teeth.

Laughing, Holmes took her hand away from the young man. "Enough, Sir Galahad. Are we going to eat or what?"

Phillip laughed as Samantha rubbed his tightly kinked, short hair.

"Aye, callan. I am a vera hungry mon, thewless, trauchled, vera peelywaly, and with an empty pechan. Gie me a break. I canna thole much langer."

None of us had a clue what the man had said but the delivery was so melodramatic that the room seemed to shake with laughter.

"What did he say?" asked Colin.

"I think he said he wants to eat." Olsen looked at his friend. "Didn't you?"

"Aye, laddie, and then some."

It was a long, leisurely, absolutely delightful lunch.

Before the gathering broke up, Lori Marie insisted that everyone present, kiss her birthmark. She wanted Samantha to kiss it twice, because the baby needed good luck too.

There were more surprises headed our way before the week was over.

Grandfather was good
Father a convicted crook
Mother took away the son
Cousin survived the scandal-
But the son sought revenge

Chapter fourteen

The Sins of the Fathers
January 20-27, 1943

At the funeral of J. B. Hobert and his 25-year-old son, Lloyd, the remaining three brothers presented a united front to the world like modern day three musketeers. The old church in Bonner Springs, Kansas was full, considering the lack of family in the area. There were no Hoberts of course, since J.B. had changed his name in 1929, replacing his family name of Alexander with his middle name. His given name of Jabar, had become J.B.

The man had opened his firm in 1930 under his new name.

There was one elderly uncle in attendance, the last living member of the Alexander family.

Faxon's fiancée, Abigail Ada Adair, was there as were two of her siblings, her parents and grandparents. Nevin's ex-girlfriend came too.

There were two dozen employees of the company in attendance, including Hector Sanchez. Of the eight men who had participated in the attack and beating of Malcolm Macdougal and George St. Giles, four had fled the city and were being hunted. The other four were in jail. All had testified that Hector had not been involved in the attack. He had subsequently been released from custody.

My brother and his wife, and Malcolm and his wife had attended the funeral. They met Sandra Rose Grun. Eric Grun had liked his employers and had been good friends with Faxon.

In the absence of George, who was in Springfield until February 18, I went along to help with John Holmes' wheelchair. William did likewise for Malcolm's.

At the graveside, Holmes noticed a slight change in the attitude of the youngest Hobert. He seemed to distance himself from his brothers after Abigail stepped up to stand beside her husband-to-be. Sandra Rose moved up to stand beside Cal.

The service finally over, people began to move away. Cars began to leave the cemetery.

Detectives Raymond and Wallace stood off to one side, to the left of our small group. He sort of saluted Holmes who raised his hand in response.

I started to turn the chair toward the car.

"Wait."

Cal Hobert was hurrying toward us, followed by Faxon and the two women. Nevin trailed along several feet behind his siblings.

Cal walked straight to Malcolm. Cal Brent Hobert, the young, cocky twenty-five-year-old, had matured overnight, faced with all the headaches and responsibilities of running a company, fulfilling all the obligations contracted for, and seeing to the welfare of his younger brothers.

The change suited him.

Cal reached for the hand of the Scotsman who had been battered by men in his employee. The shake was firm. His other hand went on top. The second shake conveyed concern and sympathy. Letting go, Cal handed the man an envelope.

"What is it, lad?"

Marian took it and opened it. In her hand she held a receipt from St. Margaret's Hospital for a paid up bill. She passed it to her husband.

"I wunna, I canna accept this, chiel." He shook his head stubbornly. He tried to hand it back to the man.

Cal and his group looked to Holmes for interpretation.

Holmes cleared his throat and obliged. "He said, 'I will not, I can not accept this, young man." He shrugged. "He is a dour fellow. Stubborn, he is stubborn."

Cal nodded his thanks. He crossed his arms and avoided the proffered receipt. "I figured you would not take the money, hence the receipt. I did the same for your partner, George. I also paid a portion of the hospital bill for the two detectives struck down with our truck. It's a done deal, Mr. Macdougal. The hospital will not return my money, I assure you."

Faxon stepped forward. "Please accept it, Mr. Macdougal. It is very important to the family."

"Gude of ye. I am donnered…dazed that ye wad gie so generously. Thank ye, lads."

Cal turned to Holmes. They shook hands. "Faxon."

Faxon stepped forward and handed Holmes an envelope. He placed it in the man's right hand.

"But?"

"Don't even think about saying no, Mr. Johnson. Dad hired you, you did your job, and here I stand, a free man about to get married."

"Can we go now? It's cold out here." Nevin looked uneasy at the approach of the two Kansas City, Kansas detectives.

Charlie stepped up to Cal. "We are sorry about your loss, Cal. We want to thank you for what you did for our friends-all of them."

"Good of you to come, detectives."

"We wanted to pay our respects," said Innes. He stepped closer to Nevin who backed away.

The expression on his brother's face alerted Cal that something was wrong. Sudden tension gripped the group.

Faxon looked from the face of Charlie Raymond to that of his brother, Cal. He looked at Nevin.

It was a dark, unrecognizable Nevin Boyd Hobert who glared back at him. All traces of the brother he knew had fled. There was an ugly, sneering meanness to this Nevin. He looked older than his twenty-one years.

"Nevin Boyd Hobert, I am arresting you for the murder of…"

Backing into Sandra Rose, Nevin knocked her down. He turned to run.

Dashing forward, Innes Wallace grabbed the young man's arm.

Nevin fought the shorter man, hitting him in the stomach with three quick blows. Innes fell to his knees but hung on to the arm. Nevin chopped at the offending arm repeatedly. Innes lost his hold, falling with a groan.

William Leonard tackled Nevin Boyd, pulling him off his feet. Charlie put his knee on the fallen man's back and handcuffed him. They pulled him to his feet.

I had jumped to the side of the fallen detective who had not gotten up. Blood had seeped through his coat sleeve, staining the snow. I began to wrap my scarf around it even as I yelled for help.

"Detective, he is hurt. His arm is bleeding. We need an ambulance. His stomach too," I added, staring at the spreading redness between the buttons of his overcoat.

"I'll call for help," yelled William as he sprinted away rapidly.

Cal and Faxon stood as though hypnotized at the unbelievable scene.

Marian helped Sandra Rose to her feet and the two women stared at the ground.

"A knife, officer. Here in the snow."

William returned, breathing hard. "On the way, sir."

"Watch him for me?"

William stepped up to Nevin and took a firm grip on his right arm.

Charlie took out his handkerchief and retrieved a short-bladed knife from the pink snow.

In the distance there was the wail of a siren.

*****

Thursday, Lee Emerson was released from the hospital and went home to his wife and daughter. He would not be back on duty for two more weeks.

Innes Wallace was in the hospital with three shallow knife wounds to the stomach, six to his left arm.

Isaac and William left town for a few days on an Insurance fraud case. They went to Wichita, the capital of Kansas.

In the absence of Veda Grantham, in Springfield for the wedding of her grandson, Julia Harrison was staying with Mollie Leonard to help with the triplets. She and Zeke Martin would marry on the 30th.

The Hobert family was fractured nearly beyond the point of recovery but the two remaining brothers stuck with it tenaciously.

Faxon's fiancée was a buttress of support for him. And what started out as a friendship between Sandra Rose and Cal, grew into a couple with a wedding in the plans.

*****

Monday January 25, the Juarez brothers were back in Kansas City to face charges for murder and assault.

Nevin was charged with two counts of murder and the assault and attempted murder of a police officer.

The young murderer stared at the two detectives sitting across the table from him, one in a wheelchair. He glanced at the detective standing at the door. The man had a cane and walked with a decided limp.

"This is detective Emerson, Nevin. Have you two met?" asked Charlie.

"No."

"Lee was working on the Judge Greene case when he and his partner were attacked by a large lumber truck. His partner is still in the hospital. It was a Hobert Company truck. We found it parked on the company lot."

"I had nothing to do with that."

Charlie drummed his fingers on the table in a slow, methodical rhythm. "Tell us about Eric Grun."

Nevin just sneered at the rumpled slate suit and black cowboy boots that Charlie Raymond wore. "Don't know what you are talking about. I didn't like him; that doesn't mean I killed him and I never touched his wife." The young killer stared unblinking at the detective. "Tell me, Mr. Wizard, what do you think I did to Eric Grun?"

"For starters, let's say you hated the man. Why did you hate him? He was out-going, friendly, competent, and honest. Why wouldn't you like a man like that?"

"Okay, I give up. Why wouldn't I like a man like that?"

"He became increasingly good friends with Faxon," said Lee. "Then, as their friendship grew, your relationship with your brother shrank. You could not stand that."

"He had two girlfriends and Eric," added Holmes. "He spent less and less time with you. You wanted Faxon to be your personal possession with no sharing."

"You forgot something, Nevin."

"What's that?"

"Faxon was your brother, a fact which would never change. You turned your love for him into an ugly, sinister, unnatural desire to possess him."

"That's preposterous. You're all crazy."

"You followed him on dates, sabotaged his car to prevent him from leaving the house, and tried to force your way into his attention. He gradually became increasingly annoyed; you became angrier." Lee stopped.

"We have witnesses and signed statements." Charlie patted the folder in front of him. "You lied to us, Nevin. You didn't break up with Janette Tomlinson. She left you."

"You scared her, Nevin, with your volatile temper striking out at her for the tiniest offense. You would pick her up for a date and end up shadowing your brother. You would forget she was even in the car. One night you cursed Eric Grun and Lucille Sloan in her presence. You threatened Janette if she did not stay quiet." Holmes shook his head, sadly. "You went too far, Nevin. It is a pity. Janette is a strong, fine girl. She would have made you a good wife."

"The nineteenth was the last straw. You blurted out your intention to end the nuisance once and for all and then compounded the error by striking Janette." Charlie took a drink of his coffee. "Shall we go on?"

The sneer had left the face of Nevin Boyd. Now it looked young and somehow vulnerable. This Nevin had a boyish innocence that made the detectives entertain a brief second of doubt.

Charlie shook his head at the direction of his thoughts.

The room was silent.

With eyes closed in the suddenly pasty-white face, Nevin began to speak in a slow monotonous voice devoid of feeling. "Yes, I did all that. I intimidated Lucille with harassing phone calls and petty vandalism. I went drinking with the Juarez brothers and we struck up a fellowship. They didn't like Eric either. I lured Eric to the station, presumably to survey a repair job. The brothers met us there. I hit him and hit him and hit him. All my hatred and anger leaped out. I was out of control. Juan pushed me away. I sat down on the roof totally spent, crying. I was mortified at first." He ran both hands through his hair. "The brothers riffled through his pockets and took his keys and wallet. Juan and I pushed him off the roof." Nevin was quiet, breathing fast and gulping air for a minute.

His face hardened and his breathing calmed. "The three of us killed that woman, Lucille. I struck the first blow." He opened his eyes. "It was exhilarating you know? It was so exciting to be doing something about my frustration. At least at first, until the reality of what I had done settled in. It's been a nightmare."

"You had no idea what kind of men you had hooked up with," said Charlie Raymond. It was a statement of fact.

"No. I did not know who they really were. If I had only known that their ultimate goal was to eradicate my family…if I had only known. If I had only had control of myself, confessed how I felt to Faxon, or Cal, or dad."

"Were you in on the attacks on Sandra Rose, or Malcolm Macdougall and George St. Giles?"

"No, Mr. Johnson." A beaten man glared at his own hands as he twisted the paper napkin to shreds. "However, I knew their intentions against Mrs. Grun but I kept quiet. I was afraid of them at this point. They were sadistic and evil. Too late, I learned it way too late." He rubbed his right temple wearily. "I didn't know she was pregnant."

"Would it have made any difference?" asked Holmes.

"No." He stopped talking.

The three detectives waited.

"Two more question," said Charlie.

"You already know everything," he mumbled.

"No, Nevin, we don't. Did you warn the Juarez brothers that your family had hired John Holmes' Detective Agency?

"Yes."

"You knew that the two beaten detectives were walking into a lion's den and could very likely be killed?"

"Yes."

"You are indirectly responsible for the attack on Mr. Johnson and his wife. She is also pregnant. Did you know that?"

He shook his head.

"I have a question," said Holmes quietly. All four men looked at him. "Which one of you was driving the truck when it struck down Detectives Vernon and Emerson?"

Nevin looked surprised.

"It's logical. The brothers had you over a barrel as the saying goes. You were deeply and irreversibly involved, like it or not. Who was driving?"

"I was."

*****

A group of very tired detectives met at Mazie's Restaurant for lunch on the 27th day of January. They joined others in a private room.

Two recovering detectives were still using canes to maneuver, but Malcolm and Lee were almost well. Innes was out of the hospital but had an arm in a sling. The wounds were shallow. Edwin Vernon unfortunately was still in serious condition.

The others that were there for the gathering were Isaac and William, and Joel and Zeke.

Herman Mazie was overjoyed. He gushed over the injured detectives until they were thoroughly embarrassed.

After ordering, the group visited for ten minutes or so before Malcolm addressed his boss. "So, callan, do ye plan to share with the rest of us? Ye wadna make us fash a' through our meal, noo wad ye?"

Eight heads turned toward Holmes. Malcolm winked.

Lee Emerson voiced a question. "What did he say?"

Holmes chuckled before answering. "Yes, Malcolm. We do plan to share, and no, we would not make you fret all through lunch."

"Okay, what does, "Noo wad ye cow-len,' mean?" asked Lee.

"Allow me, Holmes," said Innes.

"Of course." Holmes nodded at the other Scotsman at the table.

"Very simple, Lee. Noo means now, wad means would, so we have now would you, callan, question mark. Callan means young man, in this case sort of like a term of endearment. Got it?"

Lee Emerson said yes but shook his head no.

The table full of men laughed with great vigor.

Charlie Raymond raised a hand. "Well then, about Nevin."

He shared what they had gleaned from their conversations with Nevin about his association with the Juarez brothers.

"Tis a pity. A whole family nearly destroyed. I dinna see the connection between the Judge and the Juarez lads. Gude," he said as Herman and two employees entered with two carts of food. "I am vera hungry."

Plates went to everyone except Malcolm and Innes.

"Dinna tell me ye forgot us, laddie."

"Not at all, sir. We have prepared something special for you, Mr. Macdougal and for you, Mr. Wallace. A surprise for you."

Very large covered dishes were placed in front of the two Scotsmen. Herman removed the lid from Malcolm's dish and watched the hazel eyes for any sign of displeasure.

Malcolm stared at the plate of food for several seconds.

No one was eating.

"Bot, how? I am donnered. Where…?"

"We found some sheep, sir."

"What is that?" asked Charlie, eyeing the dish in front of his partner.

"Haggis," answered a stunned man.

"You need not eat it, sir," said a rather distressed Herman Mazie. I thought you would…be pleased."

Malcolm Macdougal got to his feet and hugged the startled restaurant owner. "Thank ye mightily, callant. It is a braw gesture. A bonnie treat indeed. I bood say, I am dirled… overcome. Thank ye again." He sat down.

Everyone took bites of their food but all eyes were on Malcolm. Even Innes watched him eat the first bite.

His hazel eyes closed as he savored the unique dish from his birthplace.

"Well?" asked Herman. The short man rubbed his hands nervously.

"A waly thrift. Tis been awee."

Herman looked confused.

Innes interpreted for his friend. "An excellent effort. It has been a while." He took a bite. "Vera gude, Herman. You made this?"

"Well, not exactly, sir. I got it from 'The Scotsman', the little restaurant in KCMO. You have been there?"

"Quite right. We have been there. Excellent surprise, Herman."

"Thank you, Mr. Johnson. If you will excuse me." With a slight bow, he bustled out of the room.

No one spoke. Everyone ate with gusto.

"How did you determine that Nevin Hobert was the killer of Eric Grun and Lucille? I thought he had been arrested and then released."

"Quite right, William, however, when George checked on the whereabouts of the four brothers on November 20, Nevin was not where he was supposed to be. His crew said he went on an errand for his father."

"The father had na ken of it. Did the mon cover for his bairn."

"Not at all, Malcolm. J.B. Hobert laughed it off, assuming that the boy had taken leave to see his girl friend. He had no idea what a vicious turn his youngest son's affection for his brother had taken."

"When questioned, Eduardo Juarez wasted no time implicating Nevin. He even tried to blame the boy for the kidnapping of Sandra Rose. But Juan had the key ring on him with over a dozen stolen or copied keys." John Holmes paused to taste the dessert placed in front of him. "What is this?"

"Boysenberry pie a la mode," provided Joel. "Like it, Holmes?"

"Indeed so. Quite good." He ate several more bites. "Here is another tidbit of information we picked up along the way. On November 19, Eric had called his wife on his lunch break. He mentioned going somewhere with Nevin on Friday, something about inspecting a repair job. He was fired later that day."

"He didn't tell his wife," continued Charlie Raymond. "The next morning he got a call from Nevin. Eric was told that the brothers had prevailed on his behalf and he was back on the payroll."

"It was a ploy to get him to Union Station?" asked Lee Emerson.

"Yes. He was murdered because of prejudice all right, but not for the reason Sandra thought. It had nothing to do with racial or ethnic bias."

"So, the youngest Hobert formed an alliance with two violent men with no knowledge of their intent to destroy his family?" Isaac Martin sounded shocked.

"That is correct, little brother. Nevin was using Juan and Eduardo to serve his agenda while the brothers were using him to further their goal. And all because of something that happened back in 1909."

"I don't get it, Zeke."

"Juan Roberto Juarez is Robert Brian Bartlett, son of Robert Brian Sr. and Cynthia Barrett Alexander. The five-year-old boy's world fell apart and he nurtured the grudge all his life, waiting for the chance of revenge." Zeke looked at Charlie and then at Holmes. "Or am I wrong?"

"In our research, Edwin and I found out about the sons-in-law of Thomas Alexander. His daughter, Cynthia, left her husband, moved to Mexico and eventually remarried. Their son was Robert, also known as, Juan. Sylvia's son, Jabar Hobert Horsley, became…" Lee accepted more coffee from the waitress.

"J.B. Hobert," added Innes.

"Exactly."

"Okay," said Isaac with a frown, "but why go after the Hobert's"

"Think about it, Isaac. The Alexanders are dead, the women and their husbands are dead, the building inspector was dead. Juan wanted revenge for his spoiled childhood and his mother's unhappiness, so…"

"Got it, Zeke. He went after the remaining heirs, the Hoberts and the Judge who had tried the case."

"Right, William, and Nevin Boyd Hobert played right into their hands." Holmes sat back in his wheelchair with a contented sigh. "I am full."

Charlie looked at his watch. "It is 2:15, gentlemen. We need to break this up." He stood.

"Quite right," added Holmes. "Must get back to work. This case is a sad example of visiting the iniquity of the fathers…"

"Upon the children unto the third and fourth generation, Deuteronomy 5, verse 9," added Malcolm.

"Quite right."

Like a handsome quilt
Stitching cotton, cloth and string
Into a useful pattern
Piecing scarred lives together-
Amazing art form

Chapter fifteen

Pulling it Together
January 27, 1943

"Allow me to reconstruct the morning of December 26, 1942, Juan." Charlie Raymond cocked his head toward Juan Juarez. "Or should I say, Robert?"

"I prefer Juan. What's to reconstruct? We were not at Judge Greene's mansion."

"Yes, you were."

"You and your brother loaded lumber, sand, and concrete into the bed of truck number four. At 8:20, you left the lot and drove to the Judge's house, entering by the west gate. At 8:45 you parked by the greenhouse. You went inside by the north door, Juan. Eduardo stood by the back of the truck, ready to unload. How does it sound?"

Juan shrugged. "It is your fabrication, señor."

"The Judge came outside and showed you where to put the material and then he went back inside. You and your brother unloaded, stacking everything very neatly. You went back inside the greenhouse about 10:00."

"You killed the judge," interjected Innes.

"No, señor. I collected our money."

"You hit him with a metal rod. He fell face down. You hit him again and then you reset his watch to say 12:00. You stomped on it to break it. No," said Innes. "You took his wrist and smashed the watch against the wooden plant table."

"You have quite an imagination, señor."

Charlie got up from the hardback chair he had been occupying and stretched. Innes sat down.

"Let's see now," said Charlie. "You put the metal rod by the body and dropped the sandpaper on the floor. But you also dropped something else, your invoice for the delivery you had just made. You moved the body forward, which accounts for why the sandpaper was under the dead man. Unfortunately for you, you could not reach the paper and you had to get out."

"You backed out, backing into the rope on the pulley. That is why it was on the floor. What did you do next, Juan?"

Cold black eyes stared at the detective.

"You turned on the automatic sprinkler system. It sprayed the area, effectively washing away any footprints. You stepped outside and headed for the truck.

"You are muy loco, señor."

"This is the part I like best," said Innes. "You ripped a bag of sand open and sprinkled sand over your footprints as you retreated to the grass.

"Then you pitched the half-empty bag at the stack. It landed askew, pouring out a pile of sand." Innes rearranged the sling to minimize the stress on his neck. "So, what do you think? Are you ready to confess?"

Juan Juarez stretched his long legs and snorted, looking bored. He mumbled something in Spanish that neither man recognized but had no trouble imagining what it meant.

Death in a Green House

Charlie stood at the end of the table leaning on the wall. "So, there were no footprints, no fingerprints, no one saw anyone or heard anything around 12:00 o'clock when the Judge supposedly died. Seadon Wells was a perfect patsy for the crime, although I don't believe that was part of your plan, Mr. Robert Brian Bartlett."

Robert alias Juan glared at the two detectives with a hateful intensity. "Even if I did all this, you couldn't prove it?"

"Oh, contrar, mon cher."

"There is something else." Charlie spoke softly. "If a killer approached the greenhouse at 11:50 or so, entered the greenhouse through the back door, killed the Judge, left and presumably walked or ran across a grassy field to escape..." he paused.

"Why wasn't he seen?" asked Innes. All three members of the Wells family were in the kitchen with a clear view of the green house. Mr. Lydell was cleaning off the drive around the garage. He could see the greenhouse and," Innes leaned forward, "there were no footprints. There was no way to get in and out without stepping in the sand and leaving traces on the greenhouse floor." He leaned back again. "You outsmarted yourself, foolish man."

Angrily, Juan Juarez lashed out with his handcuffed hands, striking Innes Wallace on the bandaged left arm.

Innes fell backward.

Two officers rushed into the room and restrained the violent man.

"I will never give you the satisfaction of confessing to any thing, you hear me," he shouted and tried to kick the fallen detective.

"No need, Señor Juarez. Your brother has already confessed and supplied us with details. Your goose is cooked." Charlie nodded at the two officers. "Take him back to his cell, gentlemen."

Innes Wallace was still sprawled on the floor, nursing his arm.

He chuckled as his partner helped him up. "Your goose is cooked?" Innes laughed until tears rolled from his eyes.

Charlie looked sheepish. "Come on, partner. You need some attention. Your arm is bleeding."

The two short, slightly disheveled men walked out together.

*****

January ended with the wedding of Zeke Martin and Julia Harrison, a most welcome respite from the last month's trials.

The month of February 1943 was a pleasant month, considering the ugly war raging out of sight and sound of Kansas City. It was also a busy month.

Judge Greene had decided not to sell any of his land and had made a new will. He had divided the property up into good-sized parcels, leaving equal shares to each of his children, including his daughter by Willa Uland.

Seadon married Wanda Uland and they built a house on her portion of the property. Mrs. Greene bore no ill will toward the Uland family.

George St. Giles married Georganne Hardy and she moved to Kansas City.

David Sloan remodeled the kitchen of the house his mother had died in and moved his family just in time. Charlotte was pregnant with their third child.

Faxon Hobert married Abagail Adair and the couple lived in the century-old house with Cal. Together, the remaining brothers built a thriving business.

Cal Brent Hobert, who never expected to marry, took a

special interest in Sandra Rose Grun and her coming baby. They would eventually marry. The baby would be named Eric.

Work began on the new Johnson residence but would not be completed until late April.

The war dragged on and on.

At he end of January, President Roosevelt and Prime Minister Winston Churchill, with their advisors, met in the recently recaptured Casablanca. It was a complex meeting with complex plans for future strategy.

The allies agreed to invade Sicily, Naval Chief Admiral King insisted more attention be given the war against Japan, and first priority was given to the problem of U-boat operations in the Atlantic Ocean.

There was also an agreement to launch a combined bomber offensive against Germany, from Great Britain.

There was a long way to go before the war could be declared over. A very long time.

March brought the estate family four welcome reasons for joy.

The Holmes Detective Agency worked on a dozen cases, none of which involved murder or mayhem. All were well and uninjured.

Edwin Wylie Vernon came out of his lengthy coma and started the slow road to full recovery.

Early morning March 3, an excited Jon Davis nearly broke our bedroom door as he entered with uncharacteristic vigor.

"The sir, the baby, is sir…" the tongue-tied man gestured helplessly. "Phone…Marian, the baby is coming."

"All right." I jumped out of bed and took off for the telephone, wrapping my robe around me as I ran.

"Marian, it's Patrick. It's time?"

"Yes, it's time, sir. We are loading up the car. We will be off in a few minutes. We have already called Doctor Ron." Marian laughed. "Got to go. I think it's going to be a quick delivery, sir."

I hung up and danced with my wife. Carrie laughed at my exuberance. "I'll be an uncle now. Let's go, darling." I ran for the door.

Carrie was bent over laughing at my antics.

Jon Davis stopped me just as I reached for the door handle. "You may want to dress first, Patrick."

I looked down at my robe, pajama pants and bare feet. "Quite right." I ran back to the bedroom.

By 8:00 o'clock a.m., we were on the way to the hospital. The baby was in such a hurry to arrive that our wait was short.

Carrie sat on one side of Holmes, Adele on the other. Since he could not pace the floor, I did it for him. For once, my brother did not fall asleep, as was his custom. He was much too excited.

By 9:55, the waiting room was so full that it seemed to be straining at the seams. At 10:15, Ron Cassiday entered. His freckled face was ear to ear grin, the biggest I had ever seen. His red hair fairly glowed as the light struck it. If he had had wings, he would have looked like the popular picture of an angel.

Ron walked to my brother. Holmes stood up without any help. Gripping his right hand firmly, left hand on his shoulder, the amused doctor said, "Congratulations, John Holmes. You are the father of a son. Dark brown hair, long tapered fingers and a very healthy set of lungs."

"I have a boy?"

"Yes, Holmes, a boy."

My brother wavered. Ron helped him sit down.

"Are you all right, Holmes." I dropped down beside the wheelchair.

"Absolutely, Patrick. Where's father?"

"Right here, John Holmes." Pastor John Stephens stepped up.

"You are a grandfather," he said jubilantly. At the older man's tears, he added, "Is that all right?"

"Oh yes, Holmes. It's wonderful. I wish Elizabeth was here, that's all. I just wish your mother could have been here."

For the next twenty minutes Holmes received so many hugs and handshakes that he could no longer lift his right hand.

Marian Macdougal was in tears.

Standing outside the glass wall to see a baby was becoming a common occurrence with this group but far from routine. Each child was a special and unique gift from God.

We were as excited as children at a Christmas party.

We had all stood in this exact spot to welcome my twins, my two daughters, Adele's sons, Myra Warner's baby, and now, the son of my brother and his wife, Samantha.

Aiken Oakes Ridley Johnson came home on Monday, March 8; of course, we celebrated!

Tuesday, Carrie told me that she was pregnant.

"Oh, my gosh!"

Epilogue

Holmes played his violin for the family for the first time since June 12, 1942. His partially paralyzed right arm was obviously still somewhat stiff as he laboriously rendered 'Amazing Grace'.

It was not a stellar performance, but as memorable for those who knew how much he loved playing the violin as the cry of their first-born had been. His forehead was beaded with perspiration from the concentrated effort, tears squeezing from both eyes from the tension.

As the last note sounded, my brother stopped short. His right arm fell to the cushioned stool put there for that express purpose. He lowered his instrument and bowed his head.

Everyone in that room was crying as he whispered, "Thank you, Lord."

Samantha laid their first-born son in the arms of his Godmother, my wife, Carrie, and then she went to her husband. She stood by the stool he sat on with arms wrapped around him, weeping.

The month of March was destined to land on my back like a lion, I was to be the lamb.

The End

Next book in this series of John Holmes Johnson mysteries is Death Is An Illusion

Scottish to English

a'	-	all
aboot	-	about
ae	-	a
air	-	early
alane	-	alone
allace	-	alas
ane	-	one
awa	-	away
awee	-	a little while
aweel	-	well then
aye	-	yes
bairn	-	baby, child
baith	-	both
blude	-	blood
bonnie	-	good
bood	-	must
bot	-	but
braw	-	splendid
callan	-	young man
callant	-	youngster
cam	-	come
canna	-	can not
canty	-	lively, brisk
causey	-	road, street
chiel	-	young boy
collieshangie	-	ruckus, brawl
daft	-	frolicsome
daft days	-	festive holidays
dee	-	die
didna	-	did not
dinna	-	do not, don't
dirled	-	overcome

donnered	-	stunned, dazed
donsy	-	restless, impatient
doun	-	down
dour	-	difficult, stubborn
dow	-	able to
drumbie	-	trouble
fash	-	worry, fret
fra	-	of
frae	-	from
gang	-	go
gie	-	give
git	-	get
gliff	-	brief moment, quick look
grue	-	shudder
gude	-	good
gudewife	-	wife, woman of the house
hae	-	have
haggis	-	a Scottish made with oatmeal, onions, herbs, suet, and sheep organs (heart, liver, etc.)
hale	-	well, healthy
hame	-	home
heir	-	here
ither	-	other
jimp	-	barely, scarcely
keek	-	look
ken	-	know, have knowledge of
langer	-	longer
lass, lassie	-	lady, young lady
lik	-	like
lo	-	fire
lo'e	-	love
loot	-	let

maun	-	must
manuna	-	must not
mon	-	man
na	-	no
nae	-	not
nicht	-	night
nieve	-	arm
noo	-	now
ony	-	also
oot	-	out
pechan	-	stomach
peelywaly	-	out of sorts, sickly
pot	-	put
preef	-	proof
punced	-	struck, hurt
rad	-	afraid
richt	-	right
sary	-	sorry
shouldna	-	should not
skreigh	-	yell
sonsy	-	attractive, happy
stound	-	hurt, injured
sweerly	-	heavily, soundly
syne	-	then
tae	-	to
teen	-	trouble
thae	-	those, these
tham	-	them
the day	-	today
thewless	-	weak
thole	-	to endure, put up with
thrift	-	excellent effort
trauchled	-	exhausted, tired

vera	-	very
wad	-	would
waeful	-	sad
waly	-	beautiful
wer	-	were
wun	-	will
wunna	-	will not
ye	-	you
ye're	-	your
yett	-	door